If only life were simple, Steve thought.

Ordinarily he was a man of action, always on the road. At the moment, however, living on top of this mountain had an almost irresistible appeal.

Of course, he had Victoria with him. And tiny Heidi…

How had he, a loner by choice, managed to collect not only a baby but also the sexiest woman he'd ever set eyes on? And what was he going to do with them when this mountain idyll ended?

A top-notch government agent, he'd always prided himself on keeping things under control. But now a woman and child had turned his well-ordered life into chaos.

And for once, Steve found he didn't want to plan or think about the future.

Not when he was having the time of his life…

Dear Reader,

This September, you may find yourself caught up in the hustle and bustle of a new school year. But as a sensational stress buster, we have an enticing fall lineup for you to pamper yourself with. Each month, we offer six brand-new romances about people just like you—trying to find the perfect balance between life, career, family and love.

For starters, check out *Their Other Mother* by Janis Reams Hudson—a feisty THAT SPECIAL WOMAN! butts head with a gorgeous, ornery father of three. This also marks the debut of this author's engaging new miniseries, WILDERS OF WYATT COUNTY.

Sherryl Woods continues her popular series AND BABY MAKES THREE: THE NEXT GENERATION with an entertaining story about a rodeo champ who becomes victi to his matchmaking daughter in *Suddenly, Annie's Father*. And for those of you who treasure stories about best-friends-turned-lovers, don't miss *That First Special Kiss* by Gina Wilkins, book two in her FAMILY FOUND: SONS AND DAUGHTERS series.

In *Celebrate the Child* by Amy Frazier, a military man becomes an integral part of his precious little girl's life—as well as that of her sweet-natured adopted mom. And when a secret agent takes on the role of daddy, he discovers the family of his dreams in Jane Toombs's *Designated Daddy*. Finally, watch for *A Cowboy's Code* by talented newcomer Alaina Starr, who spins a compelling love story set in the hard-driving West.

I hope you enjoy these six emotional romances created *by* women like you, *for* women like you!

Sincerely,

Karen Taylor Richman
Senior Editor

Please address questions and book requests to:
Silhouette Reader Service
U.S.: 3010 Walden Ave., P.O. Box 1325, Buffalo, NY 14269
Canadian: P.O. Box 609, Fort Erie, Ont. L2A 5X3

JANE TOOMBS
DESIGNATED DADDY

Published by Silhouette Books
America's Publisher of Contemporary Romance

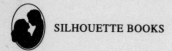 SILHOUETTE BOOKS

ISBN 0-373-24271-9

DESIGNATED DADDY

Visit us at www.romance.net

Printed in U.S.A.

Books by Jane Toombs

Silhouette Special Edition

Nobody's Baby #1081
Baby of Mine #1182
Accidental Parents #1247
Designated Daddy #1271

Silhouette Shadows

Return to Bloodstone House #5
Dark Enchantment #12
What Waits Below #16
The Volan Curse #35
The Woman in White #50
The Abandoned Bride #56

Previously published under the pseudonym Diana Stuart

Silhouette Special Edition

Out of a Dream #353
The Moon Pool #671

Silhouette Desire

Prime Specimen #172
Leader of the Pack #238
The Shadow Between #257

JANE TOOMBS

was born in California, raised in the upper peninsula of Michigan and has moved from New York to Nevada as a result of falling in love with the state and a Nevadan. Jane has five children, two stepchildren and seven grandchildren. Her interests include gardening, reading and knitting.

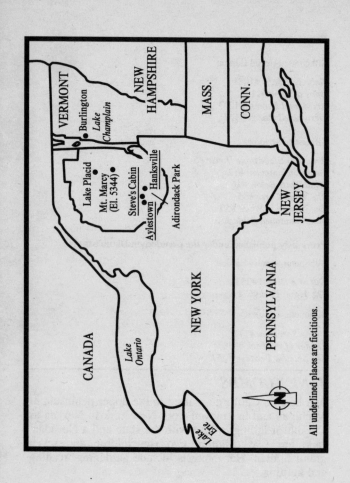

CANADA

Lake Ontario

Lake Erie

NEW YORK

PENNSYLVANIA

VERMONT

Burlington

Lake Champlain

Lake Placid

Mt. Marcy (El. 5344)

Steve's Cabin

Hanksville

Aylestown

Adirondack Park

NEW HAMPSHIRE

MASS.

CONN.

NEW JERSEY

N

All underlined places are fictitious.

Chapter One

The Capitol Beltway evening traffic was no worse than usual, but to Steve Henderson, who was coming off a tough case, coping with the rush of cars and trucks edged his tiredness into exhaustion. The strident buzz of his agency beeper was the last straw.

He had a cell phone but for security reasons never took or made agency calls on it. The beeper signal meant he had to pull off and find a pay phone to find out why he was being paged. Whatever the emergency, he was too close to crashing to cope with it. Muttering a curse, he angled toward the nearest exit, knowing it might be miles before he could work his way off.

When he finally made it, the first pay phone he located was outside. Ordinarily, outside open phone booths made him uptight, but he couldn't muster up the energy tonight. With no more than a cursory glance to right and left, he punched in the agency number.

"Fifty-one," he said into the phone, giving his code number. "What's up?"

Steve listened to the reply, frowning. "Kinnikec Hospital? What the hell for?"

Moments later, he hung up, shocked and more confused than he'd been in years. Before leaving, out of habit he put his back to the phone booth, scanning the area, but his mind wasn't on what he was doing.

The hospital. What in blue blazes had taken Kim to Kinnikec? Though it was in Maryland, the hospital was nowhere near where he thought she'd been living. They were divorced and he hadn't set eyes on her in three years so why had she given the hospital his name and the Riggs and Robinson screening phone number that led to the agency? Surprising she'd even remembered it after so long. But why call him and not Malengo?

Because she'd been Steve's wife before she took up with that slimy scumbag, the agency made it their business to keep tabs on her. She'd still been with Malengo the last he heard.

Dead. He had no choice but to go. Steve shook his head, strode to his nondescript black car and spun out of the parking area onto the access road, making his way to Kinnikec Hospital.

Knowing from experience the emergency entrance to any hospital was usually the quickest way in, Steve waited for an ambulance, lights flashing, to pull in ahead of him. By the time he found a place to park

and got to the door, the paramedics had already unloaded their patient and disappeared inside.

The front desk receptionist was on the phone and
finished the conversation before directing the man
ahead of him to go to the hospital's third floor.

"I received a call asking me to come here," Steve
said, giving his name. "They said Francine Henderson was dead and I'm listed as the next of kin."

That was another thing, he thought, as he waited
for the receptionist to shuffle through papers. Francine
had started calling herself Kim shortly after they were
married, saying she felt more like a Kim than a Francine and never permitted anyone to use her real first
name again. But here, for some reason, she had.

"If you'll step into the waiting room for a moment
I'll have a nurse come for you," the receptionist said,
her attention already shifting to the person in line behind him.

Aware that moments in hospitals often expanded
into hours, he leaned against the wall in the crowded
ER waiting room, fighting fatigue, scanning the room
from habit. No one he recognized, certainly not Malengo.

His mind couldn't take in the fact that Kim was
dead, so he shut it down and tried not to think at all.

Eventually a red-haired nurse opened the waiting
room door and said his name. Steve pushed away
from the wall. Walking toward her, he thought absently that she looked even more tired than he felt, if
that was possible.

"My name is Victoria," she said. "Please come
with me."

She led him into a small room that had the ear-marks of a sanctuary for the telling of bad news.

"I'm sorry, Mr. Henderson," Victoria said. "We did everything possible for your wife, but she died. The doctor is busy at the moment but he'll be with you soon to explain...."

Though he already knew Kim was dead, Steve was sandbagged by anguish so intense, it blotted out the nurse's words as well as everything else. He'd laid aside any feeling for Kim after the divorce—or so he'd thought—but the shock of knowing she was ir-revocably gone brought back the fact that he'd once thought he loved her. Whatever their differences, he'd never wished her dead.

Poor Kim, an orphan with no siblings. At the end there was no one to take responsibility for her but him, the man she'd left behind years before.

"I don't care to wait for the doctor," he said when he could speak. "Would he tell me anything you don't know?"

Victoria blinked, hesitating. "Not really," she said after a moment. "I was there. One of the things he would have asked you to do is make a positive iden-tification. If you feel able to, I'll show you where to go."

Dazed, caught up in remembering Kim, he had enough awareness to nod. Identification? Yes, he could do that.

Some time later, thankful to put that sad task be-hind him, again he followed Victoria, the image of Kim's peaceful-at-last face filling his mind. He as-sumed the nurse was bringing him to wherever Kim's belongings had been stored. He supposed he had as much right to them as anyone, since Malengo had never married her.

He'd neglected to tell the hospital that Kim was no longer his wife—on purpose. In the secrecy business you learn never to volunteer information. She'd had some reason for giving hospital personnel his name and, until he discovered what it was—if he ever did— he'd keep his mouth shut.

"I was with her yesterday from the time they brought her into the ER from the accident," Victoria was saying.

Steve nodded, unable to respond.

Victoria gave him a sympathetic look. "Maybe you'd rather not hear about that right now. When you want to know more, just ask me. Otherwise I'll keep quiet."

Grateful he wouldn't have to make a pretense of listening, he nodded again. He was tired to the bone and until he was able to emotionally grasp the fact of Kim's death, he couldn't process any more information.

Up they went in an elevator. When the door opened, Steve trailed Victoria onto a ward, halted when she told him to wait and leaned against the wall again, eyes closed. Mixed with other hospital sounds, he thought he heard babies crying. A shame helpless babies had to have things wrong with them, he thought. Fortunately his niece and nephew were healthy kids.

If only he could be relaxing with his sister and her family in Nevada....

Steve came back to awareness when he heard Victoria's voice. He must have fallen asleep on his feet.

"Hold out your arms," she said.

Dazedly he did as she asked and jerked to astounded alertness when she deposited a swaddled infant in his arms.

"I stayed with Francine throughout the delivery," Victoria said. "We were all thrilled when the baby came out unharmed. A miracle."

It filtered through to him that what she'd handed him was Kim's newborn baby, obviously believing he was the father.

"No, impossible," he muttered, handing the bundled infant back to her. "Impossible."

As she cradled the infant, Victoria's sympathy for Steve Henderson made tears spring to her eyes. How overwhelmed he must feel, with his wife dead, at the thought of assuming responsibility for his newborn baby. He hadn't yet had time to grieve—how could he be expected to rejoice?

"I understand," she said soothingly.

Steve shook his head as though in doubt anyone could understand.

The poor guy. Victoria blinked back tears. Though she tried to stay objective, sometimes she just couldn't. Which was why she was in such desperate need of this vacation.

Taking a deep breath, she said, "We've run the tests and kept her under observation for the required amount of time so you can take your baby home. Do you have anyone to take care of her?"

He shook his head again, looking so confused that her heart went out to him. "The baby—" he began, hesitated and didn't go on.

Though she'd sworn never to act on impulse ever

again, Victoria, remembering what she'd more or less promised the dead woman, found herself saying, "I'm on a three-month leave, starting tomorrow. If you like, I can come with you and be the baby's nurse for a few days until you're able to make other arrangements."

Steve stared at her, opening his mouth to refuse, to explain. Before the words left his lips, he changed his mind. Kim knew very well he couldn't be the baby's father yet she'd pretended to still be married to him, leading the hospital to assume the baby was his. For some reason she wanted him to protect this child of hers. From Malengo? Because odds were that scoundrel was the father.

He had to honor what amounted to her last request. At least until he dug up enough facts to know why Kim had put him on the spot. It was still hard to accept that she was dead.

"I don't know your last name," he said to the red-haired nurse.

"Reynaud. Victoria Reynaud."

"I'll take you up on your offer, Ms. Reynaud. And thank you."

"Victoria," she said. "It'll make things easier."

"Steve," he told her.

"Do you have baby supplies at home?" she asked.

"Nothing."

She raised her eyebrows but said only, "We'll have to stop and get some. A carrier-bed for safety, diapers, formula, bottles—"

"Whatever." She'd have to decide, he didn't have a clue what babies needed.

As it turned out, Steve had to make arrangements

for a mortuary for Kim as well as fill out and sign forms. When he was through he accepted Kim's belongings and followed Victoria, who was carrying the baby, out of the hospital. Ordinarily he preferred to lead but this was no ordinary occasion. Nothing in his life had prepared him to deal with Kim's death, much less her newborn child. The strangest feeling had come over him when he'd briefly held that featherweight bundle. He attributed it to panic.

His sister's children had been older when he first had anything to do with them. Under a year, but alert, active and able to communicate. This one was totally helpless. Thank heaven for the redhead.

"My car's in the parking garage," Victoria said to Steve, who didn't seem to hear her. She repeated it, adding, "Do you have a car here?"

He blinked at her as though he'd never seen her before, then nodded. "We'll go together in mine. I'll drive you back tomorrow to pick up yours."

Not is it all right if we do it this way? A statement rather than a question. She decided to give him the benefit of doubt and put it down to shock. Maybe he normally was mellower. She hoped so because she certainly didn't need to hang out with some edict-issuing jerk, even if it was for only a few days.

She'd already had her share of those types, thank you.

Considering how she'd counted the days until her much-needed leave began, she had to be a martyr for offering to help him out, she thought. The baby in her arms whimpered and Victoria sighed, cuddling her closer. No way could she have abandoned this motherless little mite without making sure the baby would be well cared for.

Steve paused beside a black sedan. She watched as his head swiveled from side to side. What was he looking for? Prowlers? The ER parking lot was safe enough. Apparently satisfied, he unlocked the passenger door and opened it for her.

As they pulled out of the lot, she asked, "Could we swing by my apartment so I can pick up a few things I'll need?"

"Not now. Buy your necessities when you shop for the baby's."

He could have spared an "okay." Victoria clenched her teeth to keep back a barbed comment. Cool it, she ordered herself. Harsh words will only upset the baby. She's the reason you're here. Ignore him.

"I'll stop by the apartment tomorrow after I collect my car," she told him, setting up her own boundary.

He grunted. After a few minutes, he said, "You mentioned an accident. What happened to Kim?"

"Kim?"

"Francine. She liked to be called Kim."

"I heard it was a two-car collision. Francine was alone in her car. I think some of the people in the other car came into the ER as accident victims, too. I was so occupied with her that I didn't pay much attention." She glanced at him. "In addition to her injuries from the accident, she was also in labor when she arrived."

"I've been working out of town. Got the call as I was coming in on the Beltway."

Which explained why his wife had been driving

herself to the hospital, she thought. But surely they'd known the baby was due to be born. How odd they hadn't prepared for it.

"You don't even have a crib?" she blurted.

He shook his head.

Well, she wasn't going to shop for a crib tonight. If she could find a carrier-type bed, that would do temporarily. Resting her head against the seat back, she closed her eyes and began a mental list of what she'd need for the baby.

The next she knew, someone was touching her arm, calling her name. She jerked awake, suddenly fearful she'd dropped the baby. Reassured that she hadn't, she said, "I must have dozed off."

Simultaneously she realized the car was parked and that she was looking at one of the big chain drugstores, open all night.

"I'll come in with you," Steve said. "You pick out the baby stuff and your overnight supplies, I'll put them in a cart and pay for the lot."

She couldn't argue with that plan. Walking into the store with him while she carried a baby made Victoria feel odd. Anyone would take them for a family, even though they were strangers to one another and she was no relation to the child. So much for outward appearances.

Her chronic fatigue made it an effort to concentrate on the baby's needs, but she finally satisfied herself that she'd gathered all the essentials. Now what would she need? After finding the basic toiletries, she located a long fits-all T-shirt that would do for sleep.

Speaking of that, she was dead on her feet. She

stood numbly by while Steve paid for the items, then followed him out to the car.

"We should unpack the infant carrier and hook it into the back seat," she said.

"That can wait. Where I live is only two blocks from here and, frankly, I need sleep."

Makes two of us, she thought as she settled herself back into the front seat. And guess who's most likely to get it? Not the person who agreed to go off with a strange man and take care of his baby.

Victoria fought to stay awake but the best she could manage was sort of a waking doze. She was minimally aware of driving through a guarded gate into a town house community and of Steve pulling the car into a garage.

He let her into the house by unlocking a connecting door and went back for their purchases. She yawned as she looked around at the modern kitchen, one that didn't look as though it had ever been used. The counters were bare of any kind of supplies or appliances.

As Steve lugged bags and boxes past her, the baby began to whimper. Thank heaven the hospital had sent one bottle of prepared formula with them, she thought as she shifted the infant onto her shoulder, making soothing sounds. All she needed to do was warm it a little.

"I need the bottle warmer," she told Steve, who paused in his back-and-forth retrieval.

"What's it look like?"

"Dump the contents of the bags on the counter and I'll show you. Please try to find the pacifier, too, while you're at it."

While she was plugging in the bottle warmer, he produced the pacifier and was holding it out when the baby opened her mouth in a full-throated wail. Steve backed away.

"What's the matter with it?" he asked edgily.

"Hungry. Or wet. Or messy. Or maybe just unhappy with leaving prebirth paradise. If you'll just go ahead and set up the infant carrier-bed in the bedroom I'll be using, I'll take care of everything else. I assume there *is* more than one bedroom."

He gave her a tired half smile. "Small, but it's there." Picking up the carrier box, he left the kitchen.

While he was putting the contraption together, Steve noticed the crying had stopped. Breathing a sigh of relief, he finished what he was doing. Postponing everything else until tomorrow, he shut his mind down, entered his own room, stripped, grabbed his pajamas pants and fell into bed, asleep almost before he hit the pillow.

He woke from a series of jumbled dreams to what he decided must be the most irritating and alarming sound in the world—the plaintive, demanding dosomething wail of an infant. Still dark, four o'clock according to the red numbers on his bedside clock. He waited for the crying to cease but it went on and on. Surely Victoria couldn't be sleeping through such a racket. But if not, she didn't seem to be doing anything to stop it.

Shaking his head, he eased from the bed and stumbled down the hall. Her bedroom door was open, her bed empty. So was the carrier-bed. Was something wrong with the baby? He found them both in the kitchen where Victoria was changing the baby's diaper on the table.

"A girl!" he exclaimed.

Victoria shot him an exasperated look. "I told you that."

She probably had. Hit with Kim's death so unexpectedly he hadn't been functioning very well last night. Apparently he'd been blind as well as deaf, because he hadn't noticed until now how attractive Victoria was. The T-shirt she wore was too big for her, but came only to midthigh, revealing most of her well-shaped legs. The front V dipped as she bent over the baby, giving him a teasing glimpse of her breasts.

He reacted predictably and cursed under his breath. Luckily the pajama bottom was loose fitting.

"Her name is Heidi," Victoria added as she finished fastening the diaper and lifted the baby into her arms. The wails faded to whimpering sobs.

"Heidi?" he echoed blankly.

"Your wife told me that she wanted the baby to be named Heidi Angela Henderson. Hadn't you discussed names?"

He hadn't a clue where the Heidi came from but Angela had been his mother's name. Touched against his will, he muttered, "Henderson?"

Victoria stared at him. "I filled out the birth certificate form that way. Why? Did Francine—Kim— use her maiden name?"

"No," he said. "I was just surprised. That babies were named so quickly, I mean."

Her eyes, an unusual color between gold and green, softened. "Your wife was critical so we needed to get as much information as she could give. I think she hung on as long as she did only to make certain she could sign the notarized papers.''

''Papers?''

''I guess you really didn't take much in last night, did you? She insisted you be appointed as the baby's guardian and so we took care of that, too.''

Steve swallowed. What was Kim trying to save this baby from? ''Wasn't appointing me guardian somewhat unusual?''

Victoria shrugged. ''Maybe. But, since you're the father, the hospital saw no problem.''

His gaze shifted from her to the infant's tiny face. It looked unformed to him, resembling no one. The fuzz on the top of her head was definitely red, though. Like Kim's. And come to think of it, Victoria's, too.

At the time of the divorce he'd vowed never to get involved with another redhead again. Now here he was with two of them. But only temporarily.

Victoria plucked a bottle from the warmer, sat down and began feeding the baby. ''Nothing to it, see?'' she said, offering him a smile. ''Fathers should learn to take care of their children early.''

''Not this early. It—she's too little.''

''Babies don't break if they're held properly. It's easy to learn—I'll show you.''

He took a step backward, shaking his head.

Victoria had to admit she enjoyed the change in him from take-charge macho guy to nervous father. All she'd noticed about him to begin with was his uptight manner, which she'd tried to forgive because of the circumstances.

Here in his kitchen, his fair hair sleep disheveled, and wearing disreputable pajama bottoms that threatened to fall off him at any minute, Steve Henderson was a far different proposition. A mondo attractive one. A blond hunk, really. Everything she didn't need in the man whose house she was temporarily living in.

There was no way on this good green earth she was going to get involved with him. The sooner he found someone else to take care of the baby, the better. Even as she thought this, her arm tightened protectively around little Heidi.

Take care of her for me, the dying woman had begged. Victoria had. She was still doing so. But it couldn't go on. Heidi had a responsible father who'd find a nurturing woman to take over in Victoria's place. Soon, she hoped.

"Think she'll be quiet after she's fed?" Steve asked.

"We can hope so. Each baby tends to have a different agenda so Heidi's is hard to predict without getting to know her better. Some simply like to cry, or so it seems."

Steve winced and glanced at the clock. It was too early to call the agency but he'd do that as soon as possible. Once they got rolling on investigating why Kim left Malengo—as she must have—he'd have some idea why she'd involved him. She'd not only named him as the father but as Heidi's guardian. He couldn't make any future plans for the baby until he knew why.

In the meantime, though he'd be responsible for Heidi, someone other than him had to assume the actual care. Victoria, who was obviously capable, was right at hand. Why replace her? The fewer people who knew about all this, the better.

Ambling back to his room, Steve told himself firmly it had nothing to do with Victoria's gold-green eyes or her tempting curves. Victoria was a nurse, the best possible caretaker for an infant. Also, weren't nurses, like doctors, trained to keep their mouths shut about patients? The last person he wanted involved in this situation was a blabbermouth.

Keeping her here was based on expediency and her attributes—and he didn't mean the ones her sleep-T had failed to conceal.

Chapter Two

Steve woke to sunlight leaking through a crack in the horizontal blinds. Nine o'clock? He never slept that late. Rolling out of bed, he started down the hall to put on the coffee, then paused, belatedly remembering he was no longer alone in the house and why. He shifted his feelings into the on-hold compartment to deal with later. Facing the problem of the present was his immediate concern.

He glanced down at his pajama bottoms, noting for the first time how worn they were, muttered, "The hell with it," and continued on. Once the coffee was dripping he retreated to the bedroom again. The next time he came out he'd showered and shaved and wore casual pants and a polo shirt.

He found Victoria, dressed once again in her hospital clothes, sitting in the kitchen holding the baby while she sipped coffee. "Not bad," she told him. "Better than the mud they brew at Kinnikec. When are we going?"

"Going?"

"To pick up my car at the hospital. If you want me to stay on till you hire someone, I have to go to my apartment and pack some clothes and things. I need my car to do that."

Before he did anything else, he'd planned to go out and call the agency from the pay phone at the convenience store outside the gates. But he could stop and call on the way to the hospital.

"I must say you keep the barest refrigerator I've ever looked into," she said.

"I'm not home much."

"Evidently Kim wasn't, either."

It was obvious she suspected something. He decided to tell her a half-truth. "Kim and I were separated. She wasn't living with me. I should have mentioned it before, but—" He paused and nodded toward the baby. "My mind wasn't functioning any too well last night."

Victoria nodded. "No, I don't suppose it was. Well, that explains the lack of baby things and the usual comforts of home here."

Bluntness wasn't something that bothered him. If she wanted to speak her mind, let her. But he didn't care to dwell on his relationship with Kim so he switched topics. "We can pick up some food while we're out."

"And eat breakfast," she said. "I don't do well on an empty stomach."

"Let's go, then."

"First you have to fix the carrier so it fits in the back seat of your car. It's unsafe for me to carry Heidi in my arms. Against the law, too."

Steve knew she was right but at the same time he had no intention of letting her take charge of his life. He drew the line where bluntness crossed over into bossiness and the sooner she realized that the better.

"I'll hook the carrier in before we leave," he said crisply. "When it comes to the baby you're the expert. Period."

Without waiting for a response he stalked from the kitchen.

Victoria stared after him. Another edict from the lord and master? No wonder his wife had left him. While pregnant, at that.

On the way to the hospital they stopped at a fast-food carry-out for a quick breakfast, eating it in the parked car. When he finished, Steve got out and made a call on the restaurant's pay phone. Once they were underway again, he began asking her more questions about Kim's accident.

"I think someone said two cars plowed into each other," Victoria said. "I was too busy to ask questions. As I recall one of the men in the other car was DOA—dead on arrival." She turned to look at the little survivor in her carrier in the back seat. As she'd told Steve, the baby was a miracle.

When they neared Kinnikec Hospital, she directed him to the employees' parking area, giving him her address and starting to explain how to get there.

He cut her off. "I'll follow you."

"We might get separated."

"We won't."

She didn't argue, merely hoping he'd get good and lost. Men who thought they knew it all were not her style. She'd had more than enough of that with dear Dr. Delmer, better known as Jordan the Jerk.

As she got out of the car, he said, "Aren't you going to take the baby?"

"No. She's asleep, she'll be fine. Why hassle with moving the carrier to my car?" Giving him a taste of his own medicine, she sauntered off without waiting for him to either protest or agree.

When she reached her car, she met Fred Nelson, a colleague from the ER just getting into his pickup, parked next to hers. "Hey, Vic," he said. "What's up? Thought you were off on burn-out leave."

"I am. But I'm temporarily taking care of that accident victim's baby for the father."

"Bummer."

"The accident, yeah. I was so busy with the woman I wasn't paying attention to anyone else. Do you know any details about what happened?"

"One dead, the other guy was torn up so bad they transferred him to Washington Hospital Center for trauma care. I heard a cop say it was a sideways collision, like maybe one of the cars was being forced off the road and swung back into the other. Baby okay?"

"Doing fine. Scaring the pants off her father. I don't think he's ever been anywhere near a newborn before."

"Yeah, well, don't let yourself get saddled with total responsibility."

"No way—it's just till he hires someone. See you in three months, Fred."

"Don't sleep it all away."

"Sounds like heaven. I might just do that." She grinned at him and got into her car.

Arriving at her apartment complex, she parked her car in its slot, noting that Steve had pulled in the driveway behind her. She might have known he wasn't the type to get lost. He got out when she did.

"She's making funny noises," he said.

Victoria opened the back door of his sedan and looked at Heidi who was waving a fist in the air but not fussing. "Nothing's wrong with her," she assured him. "Babies do make other sounds than crying."

"Don't be long."

She savored his nervousness. So much for his being macho. "Relax. Your daughter won't self-destruct before your eyes. And if she does cry, it won't hurt her."

"Maybe not, but it's painful to listen to."

"You'll get used to it," she said heartlessly, turning away toward her apartment.

By the time she returned to his car with a small suitcase, Heidi was whimpering. Victoria coaxed the pacifier into her mouth and she stopped until they parked in a supermarket lot where she began to wail in earnest.

"Now what's wrong?" Steve demanded, getting out of the car.

Victoria got out, too. "Wet and hungry, probably. I'll change her and—"

"Right here?" He sounded horrified.

"Heidi doesn't care where we are. All she wants is to be comfortable."

Steve watched Victoria's deft handling of the baby

with grudging admiration. She made it look easy. When she finished changing the diaper, she sat in the back seat with Heidi in her lap and brought out a bottle of formula. The baby sucked eagerly at the nipple.

"The other man in the accident was injured so badly, they transferred him to WHC," Victoria said to him. "Apparently one car sideswiped the other. One of the nurses on duty last night came by and told me while I was getting my car."

Steve's well-developed sense of wrongness snapped to full alert. Had the men in the second car been Malengo's? He suspected he was right. But even if Malengo wanted to get rid of Kim once and for all, he surely wouldn't kill his unborn child. Could she have been trying to escape? In that case, maybe they were trying to stop her by forcing her off the road, intending to haul Kim and the baby she carried back to Malengo.

He clenched his jaw. If that were the scenario, she must have been desperate enough to swerve into their car rather than let them capture her, making for a fatal collision.

"I'll be back in a minute," he told Victoria, striding off to the nearest pay phone to tell the agency what he suspected. They'd check on the DOA and the injured man and find out if they worked for Malengo. If they did, what could have persuaded Kim to try to escape from Malengo in the first place? He couldn't believe she'd suddenly decided, on a whim, that she didn't want Malengo to be the baby's father. He knew Kim better than that.

No, it had to be she'd discovered something that

had scared her enough to flee. Had she been trying to get to him? He'd never know for sure. Nor would he know what had panicked her. Not unless she'd had something she'd brought with her. They'd given him a bundle of what she'd been wearing and carrying. Why the hell hadn't he searched through the stuff last night?

He sprinted back to the car where Victoria was holding the baby up against her shoulder. "Put her down. We're taking off," he ordered.

"She hasn't burped yet."

"I don't give a damn. Do as I say."

She glared at him "I will not! You told me I had full responsibility for Heidi. Either that's true or you can find someone else right now and I'll take a taxi home."

Steve scowled at her, wishing he could tell her to get lost here and now. He didn't dare. Because if she carried out her threat, he'd be stranded with the baby.

"If she doesn't bring up the air she's swallowed while taking her formula, chances are she'll get a stomachache and fuss," Victoria explained. "We don't want a colicky baby on our hands."

He certainly didn't. Was there no end to the ins and outs of infant care? "Can't you carry her into the store like that while we're waiting for the great event?" he asked, deciding they may as well get the shopping over with.

"If necessary. But that's not what you ordered me to do. Which reminds me—I didn't enlist in Steve Henderson's private army. I rate requests, not orders."

Steve raised his eyebrows and she smiled sweetly.

Damn redhead. Had to admit she was right, though. When he was working, he tended to be brusque. Due to Kim's inexplicable actions and the fact she'd been associated with Malengo, this was now an agency case. They'd all like nothing better than to nail king-pin Gregor Malengo to the wall.

But he and Victoria did, after all, have time to do the necessary shopping before he went through Kim's belongings. It's just that he wasn't used to putting anything ahead of agency affairs.

"Sorry," he muttered. Apologizing didn't come easily to him. "I'll try to remember you're a volun-teer, not a recruit."

"A temporary volunteer," she reminded him.

As they entered the store, he thought what a strange threesome they made. No doubt to the casual ob-server, the reluctant nonfather, the temporary nurse and the motherless baby looked to be a family. A happy family? The idea made him smile wryly.

Victoria picked out far more food than he could imagine them needing but he kept his mouth shut, aware he had no expertise in basic meals. Carry-out and microwavable food he could comment on but nothing prepared from scratch. Made it a tad awkward when he visited his hideout in the Adirondacks—but he didn't get up there too often.

She chose other baby items, too, which he paid little attention to.

At the checkout, the baby not only burped audibly but spit up a glob of milk on Victoria's shoulder, which was luckily protected with a cloth. Babies seemed to be messy little things. He admired Victo-ria's competence. She was a known factor, as well.

At his request the agency had run a check on her and she'd come up clean. Usually best to deal with what you had rather than the unknown. He'd convince her to stay on until he knew what to do about Heidi Angela Henderson.

They got back to the condo and unloaded the car without any surprises from the baby, who seemed quite content in the carrier, though awake. He set the carrier carefully in the middle of the table and started to leave the kitchen.

"Wait, please," Victoria said. "I'll need some help getting this on."

She'd stressed the *please,* making it a definite request—for his benefit. He acknowledged her ploy with a reluctant smile.

The help she needed from him was in fastening some kind of contraption around her, sort of an up-high kangaroo pouch evidently designed to carry a small infant in. This required him to get close enough to her so her scent—something pleasantly floral—filled his nostrils. He quashed a vagrant impulse to move closer still.

Keep your distance, Henderson. Whatever she has, you don't need. Like you told her, she's the baby's nurse. Period.

"Thanks," she said.

"My pleasure," he surprised himself by saying. Surprised her, too, from her expression. But, what the hell, it had been a pleasure.

Enough of that. Back to business. Past time to go through Kim's belongings. He turned away to do just that.

"Oh, damn," Victoria said.

Steve whirled around. "What's wrong?"

"I forgot something important. I don't go any-where without what I call my medical survival kit. I left it in the trunk of my car."

"You mean a first-aid kit?"

"No, a lot more than that. It's important that I have it here because of the baby."

Steve frowned. Here he'd been silently approving Victoria's competence, and now she was turning out to be as forgetful as the next woman. He was not a fan of disorganization.

"We need to go back and get it right away," she went on. "I don't want to discover I need something from the kit and not have it on hand."

He couldn't deny she might need the damn thing—what did he know about babies?—but there was no way he was going to haul her and Heidi back to her apartment complex.

"Give me your car keys and I'll run over and get the kit from your trunk. What's it look like?"

She told him as she handed him the keys.

Her so-called survival kit turned out to be exactly where she'd told him it was. After relocking the trunk of her car, he stowed the kit in his car and started for home. Even though he didn't expect to be followed, out of habit he took a roundabout route designed to detect such a problem. On the fifth turn, he noticed the same brown car was still behind him.

Why would any car take this convoluted route he'd chosen unless they were following him? Unlikely as it seemed, he'd picked up a tail. Working for the agency had taught him it paid off to be a bit paranoid.

Now he'd have to lose the brown car because no way did he intend to let it follow him home.

Where he lived was as much of a secret as he could make it. He'd moved after Kim left him, and had taken care she never learned his new address. He sure as hell didn't mean to lead anyone there.

Malengo? He nodded. No one else had any reason to be on his tail. Odds were the driver of the brown car was his man. What was Malengo looking for? Kim's baby? Something incriminating that had been in her possession? Or both?

Damn. He could and would lose the brown car, but that didn't mean someone with Malengo's resources wouldn't ferret out where he lived. Anger hammered through him. Kim had gone to great lengths to keep her baby from Malengo, but once the man discovered the baby's location, Heidi would no longer be safe.

Using a few tricks he'd picked up during his agency years, he soon ditched the tailing car. Even then he didn't drive directly to the complex but weaved around it several times to make certain it was safe to drive through the gates. All the while he kept puzzling over how Malengo could have made the connection between him and Victoria. Because her apartment was where he'd picked up the brown car. Obviously Malengo had it staked out.

The leak had to have come from Kinnikec Hospital. Malengo would have been notified that one of his men had died there, even though the injured one had been transferred to Washington Hospital Center for treatment. It wouldn't have taken him long to send someone around to both hospitals asking questions. Victoria, with her red hair, was easily identifiable.

He was lucky he hadn't been tailed earlier. Or had he? Not to his knowledge, but... Better play safe and see what the agency had dredged up. Steve swerved into a convenience store and grabbed the pay phone. Minutes later he flung himself back into his car, his suspicions confirmed. The DOA brought into the Kinnikec ER had been a known Malengo employee. So was the victim who'd been transferred to Washington Hospital Center.

His scenario had been right on target. Malengo must have sent the two men in pursuit of Kim, with orders to bring her back. Her desperation to avoid capture had probably caused the accident. The remaining mystery was why she'd been trying so frantically to escape Malengo.

Once through the gates, he turned into his street with adrenaline pumping, no longer certain the town house was safe. If it was, he'd made up his mind what to do. If not—he'd take things as they came.

Gun in hand, he activated the garage button and drove in, scanning its interior bareness before letting the door down. Exiting the car, he moved cautiously toward the connecting door to the house, then unlocked it quickly, slamming it all the way open.

The door smacked into the wall. Victoria, sitting at the table eating a sandwich, let out a squeal and the baby in her pouch began to cry.

Hastily shoving the gun out of sight, Steve entered the kitchen. "Sorry," he muttered.

"Do you always come in like a March lion?" she asked tartly.

Since she didn't mention it, apparently he'd been

quick enough so she hadn't seen the gun, something which he was grateful for.

"Door got away from me," he told her. "Have you unpacked?"

"No, not yet," she said. "Why?"

"Good, because we're leaving right away for the cabin."

Victoria stared at him. "The cabin?" she asked. "Where's that?"

"In the mountains. I've decided the peace and quiet will be better for the baby. For all of us. Didn't you tell me you're supposed to be on vacation? So am I, and that's the place I'd like to spend it."

"Caring for Heidi was supposed to be only for a few days," she said.

"You mean you'd turn down a paid vacation in the Adirondacks?"

He couldn't know it but he'd hit on her dream. When she was ten and her parents were living in New York, she'd been sent to a summer camp in the Adirondacks. Her stay there had been the most wonderful six weeks of her life, before or since. She'd always wanted to visit those mountains again but never had the chance. As she weighed his offer, she gently rocked Heidi back and forth in the pouch until her wails subsided.

"You frightened the baby," she accused, stalling for time.

"Didn't mean to. You know I don't like to listen to her cry. We need to hurry if we're going to get there before midnight."

"You're assuming I'm going."

His gaze challenged her. "Do you plan to leave me alone with the baby?"

He knew damn well she wouldn't do that; he was pushing her buttons again. Unfortunately they were the right ones. And he *had* said paid. Which had been implicit from the beginning but not confirmed in so many words. Plus she'd be in her dream mountains.

She stood up and looked at him levelly. "I'll come as Heidi's caretaker. Period."

His mouth twitched as though he fought a grin. "No sex? Well, I can stand it if you can."

Just when she pegged him as humorless, he fooled her. Victoria gave him a reluctant smile. "I'm not known for changing my mind."

"Neither am I."

"Since we agree, I'll pack Heidi's things."

"Groceries, too, including staples. I don't keep edible supplies on hand up there."

"Please," she reminded him.

He crooked an eyebrow but she held his gaze until he muttered, "Please."

As Victoria began gathering up the baby's clothes and other necessities, she assured herself her decision to accompany Steve to his mountain cabin wasn't rash. True, she tended to be impulsive, but since she'd never been drawn to his type of man—domineering, aloof and uncommunicative—there'd be no "vacation romance" to regret later.

Though eventually she'd have to leave Heidi, she was happy to have the chance to be with the baby longer. Because they'd bonded, it'd be a sad time for her when they parted for good. Fortunately that wouldn't apply to Heidi's father. When she and Steve parted ways there'd be no weeping on either side.

After her devastating experience with Jordan the Jerk, she'd thought a lot about what she wanted from a man. Mere sexual attraction wasn't nearly enough. He'd be a person she could trust because they shared their true feelings with one another and he'd be totally empathetic. She doubted that Steve had even one empathetic bone in his body.

"I'm agreeing to this for you," she crooned to Heidi. "For you and for me."

In his bedroom, folding clothes into his bag, Steve heard her words and smiled wryly. He had no illusions about why Victoria was going to the cabin with him. Just as well she'd warned him off sex because it set up the rules ahead of time. Not that he'd planned to romance her. One thing to admit he was attracted to her—another redhead, of all women—and completely another thing to plan to act on that attraction.

The only problem was, in banning sex, she'd set up a challenge. Unfortunately, he'd spent his entire life thriving on challenge, a habit he might find difficult to break.

Chapter Three

Although she was eager for her first glimpse of the Adirondacks, Victoria dozed off and on during the drive to New York. Which was easy to do because Heidi was also sleeping and Steve wasn't the world's greatest conversationalist. He seemed to be rationing each word.

She roused from one of her naps when he said, "Aylestown at last. Here we are in the upstate New York boondocks, Victoria."

Looking around she saw they'd stopped in a small community in front of what appeared to be a residential garage.

"We change to the van here. Need it for the mountain roads," he said before getting out and unlocking the garage door.

Inside was a four-by-four gray van, not new nor

old, unremarkable in every way, like his car. After he backed it out, Victoria helped him transfer their belongings and supplies and then held the baby while he shifted the carrier to the van.

"The carrier's only a temporary solution for a baby bed," she said. "You really should think about getting a crib or a bassinet for her."

"There's an old cradle at the cabin. You can buy some gear for it."

Accustomed by now to the way he expected her to handle everything concerning the baby, she didn't really believe he'd have any idea of the cradle's dimensions. "What size is it?" she asked anyway.

"Standard, I assume."

Victoria nodded resignedly. With an old cradle, that meant nothing, but she'd do her best. At least Heidi would have a real bed. She wondered whether Steve and Kim had chosen the cradle together during happier days.

As if in answer, he said, "I bought the cabin furnished. The cradle came with it. Never expected to use the thing."

"But it *is* usable?"

"Seems sturdy enough. She doesn't weigh much."

"Seven pounds, three ounces at birth."

Steve gazed assessingly at Heidi. "Puny little thing."

Victoria bristled. "That's a normal birth weight. She's a beautiful baby."

"I'll take your word for it."

He'd never once asked to hold his daughter. She wondered when he would. Or maybe it should be *if* he would. First-time fathers were often nervous about the fragility of newborns but he seemed unwilling to have anything to do with his daughter. She'd wait until they were settled into the cabin and then make an effort to get him acquainted with Heidi.

Once the van was packed, he drove the black car into the garage, closed the door and locked it. "We'll stop at the chain store outside of town and pick up everything we might need in the next week or so," he said when he got into the van. "Not easy to go shopping once we're there."

Duly warned, Victoria stocked up on disposable diapers, formula and more clothes for Heidi as well as pads, sheets and blankets for the cradle—plus extra food. They ate in the fast-food place inside the store and there Victoria fed, burped and changed Heidi.

Once on the road again, shortly after they left the town, they started to climb. Steve soon turned onto a secondary road, rounded a curve and stopped.

She glanced at him, eyebrows raised.

He bent forward, fiddling with the odometer. "Always mean to check the mileage going up," he muttered. "Keep forgetting."

The distinct impression he was fudging made her uneasy. Still, if the odometer wasn't the real reason he'd stopped, what could be?

Several cars passed before he eased back onto the blacktop. After a while he turned again, this time onto a narrow gravel road that wound its way up a mountain. Evergreens grew close on each side, their aromatic scent filtering into the van.

Victoria took a deep breath. "I can't believe I'm really in the Adirondacks after all these years."

"You've been here before?"

"Once." She smiled at the memory as she told him about her childhood camp days. "It's one of the reasons I agreed to come to your cabin," she added. "Heidi's my main reason, though. I think she needs me."

He slanted her a look she couldn't quite interpret. "You won't mind the isolation, then," he said finally.

"You make it sound as though your cabin is perched on the mountaintop with nothing around except trees. Like you're king of the hill."

He half smiled. "Not a bad feeling. Happens there's one other cabin about a half mile away, but she won't bother us."

Determined to pry more out of him, Victoria echoed, "She?"

"Old woman named Willa Hawkins. Harmless."

Harmless. What a strange way to put it, since the same could be said of most old women.

"Keeps to herself," he added.

"Is this the only access road?" she asked as they drove around yet another switchback.

He nodded. "There's a foot trail down to a hamlet called Hanksville on the other side, but no road from the cabin to there."

Belatedly she realized such isolation might mean primitive living. Come to think of it, she hadn't noticed any electric poles climbing with them. "How about lights and water?" she asked.

"I tapped a spring so water's no problem. Got a windmill pumping it into a tank. Kerosene lamps. Could get a generator but they're noisy. I like the quiet up here."

"Uh—toilets?"

"I had a septic tank put in. Kept the outhouse for emergencies." He glanced at her. "Think of it as an adult camp."

Which was okay with her, but caring for a newborn on top of a mountain with no electricity might prove to be a challenge. Still, she looked forward to her time at Steve's cabin. Not because of him, although she was more aware of him next to her than she wanted to be. He really was an attractive man and, despite his wary, keep-out attitude, she felt drawn to him.

Was it because he'd suffered a loss? She'd been told often enough she was too empathetic for her own good. He and Kim had separated, but he must be emotionally distraught over her death and maybe blaming himself for not being more understanding.

Victoria grimaced. No, that was going too far. Though she believed Steve mourned his wife's death, he certainly didn't act as though he felt guilty about anything.

"If you ever feel you want me to tell you more about Kim's last few hours," she said, "I will."

"Not at the moment."

From the tone of his voice, she was surprised he hadn't added *Period.* Sooner or later, she knew he'd ask, though. Survivors almost always did.

Look, she warned herself, don't get caught in the offering-comfort trap. He's enough of a hunk so it could turn physical, and that's the last thing you need from this guy. You're the baby's nurse, not his. Reserve your nurturing for Heidi while enjoying the mountain air and scenery, but leave the father alone.

Steve had kept his cabin to himself for so long that he felt uneasy bringing another person into his hideaway. Two, if he counted the baby. Fortunately she was too little to be aware of her surroundings. Victoria, though, was an adult. And too damn appealing for her own good. Or his.

He hadn't been this kind of aware of a woman for a long time. She set him on edge, wanting to touch her and knowing anything like that was out.

Bad enough he'd been forced to allow her into his secret sanctuary. He'd never brought anyone here before; no one knew about the cabin. He'd never told Kim—or anyone. Even the agency. If no one knew, then it was his safe place, his and his alone. But now Victoria would know.

Should he have thought twice? He shook his head. Kim's baby had to be kept away from Malengo until he knew all there was to know about Kim's death. Taking Heidi to his sister in Nevada had crossed his mind, but it wouldn't be fair to involve Karen and her family in a situation that could prove to be dangerous. He could be traced to Nevada.

There was no danger here for anyone. The innocent baby and Victoria, the innocent bystander, were perfectly safe. He'd made certain he hadn't been followed here; no one could discover his whereabouts during the time the agency worked on the case.

"I noticed you unpacked Kim's belongings before we left," Victoria said. "I think you should know that some of her clothes weren't salvageable."

He nodded. He'd found nothing relating to Malengo among her things and thought it was unlikely there'd been anything in the clothes the hospital had disposed of. Whatever Kim's intent had been, her reason for fleeing from Malengo remained a mystery. For now.

"How long do you plan to stay in the mountains?" Victoria asked.

Since he could hardly tell her until it was safe to leave, he said, "A week, two, possibly a month."

He wondered what her reaction would have been if he'd said, "As long as I can keep my hands off you."

She bore no resemblance to Kim, even though they were both redheads. Kim had always tried for a certain edgy elegance, Victoria was casual. Easy to be with, for all her bluntness.

When the shock of the divorce had worn off, he'd realized life was more comfortable without Kim around and that his distress was more due to the marriage failing than to his missing Kim. He didn't accept failure in himself and only reluctantly in others.

Kim had never understood he had the kind of job in which he absolutely couldn't talk about his work. She'd complained that he didn't talk about anything else, either—which might have been true, especially since they didn't share many interests.

Driving up here, Victoria had gone to sleep rather than starting meaningless conversations. Which suited him just fine. There was no need for them to try to get to know one another. Wiser not to be friendly. Neutral was the best choice.

If only she wasn't so damn good to look at. It was like having his favorite raspberry pie in front of him and trying to convince himself he wasn't hungry.

He glanced in the rearview mirror, this time at the baby instead of watching for any following car. None were; he'd made certain of that. Heidi's arms waved in the air as she made unintelligible sounds. He realized he had no idea when babies began to say actual words.

Was she able to recognize Victoria? Or was her caretaker just a meaningless face? Not that it made any difference—he was merely curious.

"Do you think she knows you?" he asked.

"Heidi? Yes, she probably knows my voice and my face by now. Infants pick up on this very early. I'm not so sure she's aware of you yet, though."

For some inexplicable reason, this bothered him. He had no intention of getting attached to Kim's baby, so why did he care? "Because I'm a man?" he asked.

"Not at all. If you'd taken care of Heidi from the beginning, she'd know your face and voice. As soon as you begin to talk to her and hold her, you'll be familiar to her, too. You're her father. She needs to get to know you."

Impossible to explain to Victoria. The truth wasn't his to give away. Secrets within secrets had been his way of life for so long, he'd almost forgotten what it was like to speak the truth without caring who heard.

He rounded the last curve and the cabin came into sight. Its rustic exterior, dark wood that blended into the surroundings, never failed to soothe and relax him. It was one story, though the sharply peaked mountain roof had made possible a sleeping loft reached by a spiral staircase.

Since there was a bedroom downstairs he'd never used the loft. Now he'd be sleeping up there.

"Perfect!" Victoria exclaimed. "Your cabin looks as though it grew here."

He grinned at her, pleased by her perceptive remark.

She smiled back, her green-gold eyes sparkling, looking as enticing as the most delicious raspberry pie in existence. Damn, but he was hungry.

"I can't wait to see the inside," she told him as he pulled the van into the attached carport he'd built himself last year.

He'd grown accustomed to thinking about the baby first and so, while Victoria held her, he unhooked the carrier and brought it into the cabin, setting it in the center of the pine table.

Victoria, following him with Heidi, zeroed in on the maple cradle by the fireplace and set it to rocking gently with her foot. "A high cradle," she said. "I didn't realize they made them in the old days— charming and practical. If you'll bring in what we bought in Aylestown first, I'll fix up the cradle for her—after I wash it."

By the time he'd hauled in all the supplies, Victoria had settled Heidi into the cradle, where she looked to be right at home amidst the colorful new bedding. He had a strange feeling he'd never be able to see the cradle again without picturing this baby in it.

"You have mice," Victoria announced.

"The curse of unoccupied wilderness cabins," he acknowledged, pleased she took the news so calmly. "I came prepared."

She nodded and continued washing down the shelves of the small pantry, adding, "I can see the reason for all these lidded metal containers. Mice-proof.''

Dusk had begun to settle in around the cabin, so he prepared and lit the kerosene lamps, then started a fire in the woodstove. Since the cabin's main room was open—kitchen, dining and living space in one—the stove would offer sufficient heat for the cool night to come.

''What runs the refrigerator?'' Victoria asked. ''I see it's working.''

''Butane.''

She nodded. ''You put my things in the bedroom down here so I assume that's where I'm to sleep.''

''I'll be up in the loft,'' he assured her.

Her glance told him she'd assumed that. ''I've cleaned my bed and put new sheets on,'' she went on, ''but the loft's up to you. I'd like you to help me move the cradle near my open door because as soon as Heidi's asleep I'm going to crash.''

Once she was in bed, he'd have to go past that open door to get to the only bathroom, situated next to the kitchen because the plumber had decided that was the best solution for the pipes.

Go past the open door, not enter.

''Is it safe to leave these lit all night?'' Victoria asked, gesturing at the kerosene lamps.

''I don't.'' He reached into the pantry where the extra flashlights were stored and handed her one. ''Use this if you need to get up while it's dark.''

''Like camp used to be,'' she said with a smile. ''I feel like a ten-year-old kid again.''

You sure as hell aren't built like a ten-year-old, he was tempted to say as his traitorous mind flashed a mental picture of Victoria as he'd seen her in her sleep-T. Down, Henderson, he warned himself. She's off-limits.

Victoria thought she'd sink into sleep as quickly as she had the previous night but it eluded her. Maybe all those catnaps in the car hadn't been such a good idea. She lay listening to Steve moving around in the outer room, then heard him climb the stairs.

When she began to imagine him stripping and pulling those disreputable pajama bottoms over his nakedness, she stopped short. None of that. As a nurse she'd seen more naked men than she cared to count. This one couldn't be much different, so why was she getting herself in a tizzy over him?

So, okay, they were together in a romantic mountain cabin—alone, if she didn't count the baby. But a newborn wasn't old enough to be any deterrent to two adults. Consenting adults? She shook her head. Hadn't they agreed, at her insistence, there'd be no sex?

If they hadn't, would she want to make love with Steve? Victoria sighed. To be honest, yes and no. She found him sexy despite her reservations about his personality, but even if she were totally wacko over him, which she wasn't, there was no way she intended to get involved with a man still nursing his grief for his dead wife. Bad idea.

Besides, she didn't know him well enough.

Relax, girl, and enjoy your paid mountain vacation, she told herself. He doesn't expect anything for his money except good care for his daughter, and that is damn well all you're going to offer.

The next morning, once she'd eaten and Heidi had

been taken care of, her fascination with the mountains drove her outside. The crunch of an ax biting into wood led her around to the back where Steve was chopping a dead tree into stove-length chunks.

His shirt hung on the branch of a sapling and his naked chest gleamed with sweat. A lock of fair hair hung distractingly over his forehead. Old, well-fitting jeans completed the picture of a wilderness he-man. A gorgeous one. Any woman would react, she consoled herself when she felt her pulse speed up.

"Heidi's asleep," she told him. "I'm going to take a short walk. Don't worry, I'll stick to the trail like a good camper so I won't get lost."

Steve rested the ax head on a log and brushed back the errant strands of hair. "What if she wakes up and cries while you're gone?"

"I won't be long. Anyway, it doesn't hurt a baby to exercise her lungs now and then. If you want to, you could pick her up. Babies like to be held."

He shook his head. "She doesn't know me well enough."

"I'll introduce you when I get back." Victoria's voice was tinged with laughter. The mountain man was afraid of a seven-pound infant.

She set off on a trail leading away from the front of the cabin, enchanted by the woodsy scents, the pine needles underfoot and the relative quiet. Soon the muted chop of the ax faded and the only sounds were the occasional cry of a blue jay and the scuffle of her footsteps through the dried needles.

After a time, she caught a flash of red to her right and stopped, staring in delight as a fox slipped through the underbrush and disappeared. His passage flushed a large bird from hiding. A partridge of some kind? She stepped off the trail for a better look at it.

The next she knew she was falling. Her surprised scream was cut off abruptly when she thumped down hard on a rocky ledge. After she caught her breath, she tried to sit up and take stock, only to gasp at the sudden shock of pain in her left shoulder. It hurt so much, she was gripped by a wave of dizziness that forced her to lay back and close her eyes.

After the pain subsided enough so she could think, she cautiously opened her eyes and found herself looking into the wrinkled brown face of a dark-eyed woman.

"Don't fash yourself none, girl," the woman said. "I'm here to help. Where're you hurt?"

"My left shoulder," Victoria told her.

"Broke, maybe?"

Victoria ran her right hand carefully over the injured shoulder. "I don't think so."

"Good. I'll just give you a hand up, then."

Belatedly it dawned on Victoria who the woman must be. "Are you Ms. Hawkins?" she asked.

"Plain Willa'll do." The old woman reached a hand down to her.

Moments later, a shaken Victoria stood beside Willa on the trail, supporting her left arm with her right one because the shoulder didn't hurt as much that way.

"Wrenched it pretty bad, did you?" Willa asked.

Victoria nodded. "I shouldn't have left the trail without taking more care."

"I figure the secret man brought you up here with

him, something he never did before. Must be you're special.''

The name fit the man perfectly. "If you mean Steve Henderson, I'm taking care of his baby. My name's Victoria Reynaud.''

"That's who I mean. Keeps to himself. Baby, huh? Never knew he so much as had a wife.''

"She died.''

Willa shook her head. "Here I stand blathering away while you're hurting. Come on, I'll fix you up best I can.'' The old woman started off in the opposite direction from the cabin.

"Wait,'' Victoria called.

"My place is closer'n his,'' Willa told her.

After a brief hesitation, Victoria followed her, figuring Willa probably knew as much or more about first aid as Steve. Not that anything would help a whole lot—the injured shoulder would have to heal by itself. What a stupid thing to do, she thought.

Willa's cabin was smaller and looked a good deal more weather-beaten than Steve's. Several outbuildings flanked it, and a tiny garden, surrounded by a fence, flourished in a space cleared of trees.

Once inside, a variety of sharp, distinct odors assaulted Victoria. She traced them to what she recognized as drying herbs hung from lines running across the main room of the cabin.

Willa gestured her toward a tall stool and began rummaging in a cupboard. "Here 'tis,'' she said at last. "Thought I had some left.''

She crossed to Victoria, a white jar in hand. Taking off the lid, she set jar and lid on the counter, then very gently pushed up the sleeve of Victoria's T-shirt and examined her left shoulder.

"Like you thought, not broke," she said. "'Tisn't cut open, but bruised some. My ointment'll help with that 'n' ought to lessen the pain. Make it myself. Some folks set such store by it, they climb clear up the mountain from Hanksville to buy the salve from me."

Whatever was in it couldn't hurt her, Victoria decided, and allowed Willa to smear the brownish ointment onto her shoulder, appreciating the cool feel and the gentleness of the old woman's hands.

When she finished, Willa fetched a length of cloth from a drawer and fashioned a sling to support Victoria's left arm.

"That ought to do it," she announced. "Feeling better, are you?"

Victoria nodded. "Thanks for your help. A paramedic couldn't have done any more than you have."

Willa grinned, revealing several gold teeth. "My people were healers. 'Tis in the blood. Want me to walk you back to your cabin?"

"I think I can make it okay. It was really lucky for me you happened along when you did."

"Wind blows this way, carries sounds. I was out picking simples 'n' heard that screech you let out when you fell."

As Victoria slid off the stool, from nowhere, a huge gray cat appeared and sniffed at her ankles. "We could use you to scare the mice away," she told the cat.

"Can't give up Tansy Ann," Willa said. "You're

welcome to her kit, though. Only one this time. She's getting old, like me.''

"Well, thanks, but I don't know how—''

"Don't you worry none about Mr. Henderson. I'll come by to see how you're doing 'n' bring the kit then. 'Tis a tom, name of Bevins.''

Deciding to let Steve deal with Willa, Victoria didn't argue.

Treading carefully along the trail leading back to Steve's cabin, Victoria told herself her fall had not only been stupid but unnecessary. She'd meant to keep to the trail and certainly should have. There was no excuse for being careless. Now her sore shoulder was sure to hamper her care of Heidi.

What would Steve say? Nothing complimentary, she knew.

But she wasn't Heidi's mother, she never would be. The tears she'd successfully blocked before filled her eyes and rolled down her cheeks.

Chapter Four

Victoria heard Heidi's wails before she came in sight of the cabin. She hurried her pace, but having one arm in a sling disturbed her balance enough so she didn't dare risk running. The last thing she needed was another fall.

Steve met her at the open cabin door. "What the hell happened to you?" he demanded, eyeing the sling.

Brushing past him, she tossed, "I fell," over her shoulder. In the cradle a red-faced Heidi cried furiously. The smell in the immediate vicinity told Victoria why.

"She needs her diaper changed," she told Steve who was hovering over them both.

He sniffed the air and grimaced. "Is that all?"

"You'd complain about it, too, if you were a baby. In fact, you probably did."

Feeling it was risky to try to pick the baby up one-handed, Victoria slipped her left arm from the sling and started to lift Heidi. Pain shot through her shoulder, making her groan involuntarily and abort the attempt.

"What's the matter?" Steve asked as she eased her arm back into the sling.

"I can't lift her. It hurts too much. You'll have to pick her up for me."

"Me?" Steve's aghast look would have amused her if her shoulder wasn't throbbing so painfully.

"You." Pain sharpened her voice. "You're her father, aren't you? It's simple. Slide one arm under her to support her head—newborns don't have any strength in their neck muscles—and lift her up, cuddling her against your body. I've heard some men compare it to holding a football."

"A football?" He sounded incredulous.

"Whatever. Just do it."

Scowling, Steve bent over the cradle and hesitantly eased his arm under the crying baby. His fingers curled around her tiny head, he cautiously lifted her and held her against him.

"If you'll carry her to that little table over there that I've padded with a blanket, I'll help you change her," Victoria said.

"Help *me?*" Outrage roughened his voice. Heidi wailed louder.

"Look, I'm not going to be able to use my left arm for a few days. I'm sorry, but that's the way it is.

You'll have to learn to care for your daughter until I can take over fully again."

The fact Heidi wasn't his daughter didn't make any difference at the moment. His problem was that she was so little, he was afraid of hurting her. Plus having to handle a messy diaper. He'd been forced into a lot of frightening and dangerous situations in his life but never had he expected to be faced with this.

With exaggerated care, he walked across to the changing table and awkwardly deposited the baby onto it. "Now what?" he muttered.

Victoria told him. In minute detail. When he finished, she said, "Credible, but the clean diaper is so loose, it won't stay on her. Tighten the tabs."

Hesitantly he did, worrying he might get them too tight and injure the baby. Heidi, who'd continued crying throughout his performance, eased into whimpers when he lifted her again. With Victoria's encouragement, he arranged the baby up against his shoulder and then even the whimpering stopped.

"She likes to be held," Victoria pointed out. "It's a characteristic need in all humans that we never quite outgrow."

Despite his acute distaste for diaper changing, a glow of satisfaction enveloped him. What he'd done had made the baby stop crying. He hadn't, as he feared he might, harmed any of her vital parts, and now she was content to have him hold her.

"I can warm a bottle of formula one-handed," Victoria said. She nodded her head toward an old oak rocker. "That seems to be the best place to feed her."

He frowned. "Surely you can feed her with one hand."

"If I have to, yes. But I think it's important for you to learn basic infant care here and now so that if anything happens to me, you can take over. Though my fall was caused by my own carelessness, it may have been a blessing in disguise, showing us why you need to be able to do what's necessary for your daughter."

Her logic was inescapable. Since he'd taken the responsibility for Kim's baby, whether he wanted to learn or not, basic care of Heidi went along with the deal.

Easing into the rocker, he said resignedly, "Bring on the bottle."

While he fed Heidi, without intending to he gazed intently into her face. At first her blue eyes seemed to focus on him but, as she sucked on the nipple, they gradually drooped shut. No longer did she seem merely a blob to him but emerged as a tiny person. He decided she had Kim's chin as well as her blue eyes and red hair.

"Did Kim see her before she died?" he asked abruptly.

Victoria nodded, her expression conveying sympathy without words. It made him feel like an imposter. While he regretted that Kim had to die, he didn't grieve for her as a man would for a wife he'd loved and lost. Their marriage had been over even before she left him for Malengo, though that had been the impetus that propelled the divorce.

But there was no way he could explain all this to Victoria. In any case, their contact was only temporary. She'd be better off believing what she did now until she left him. Left his employ, he corrected, dismissing the uneasiness that infused him when he thought about Victoria being gone.

"The nipple's fallen out of her mouth," Victoria pointed out.

"She's asleep. That's why."

"Time to burp her."

"She'll wake up," he protested.

"Remember what I told you about air bubbles?"

He did. They went with colic. Setting the bottle aside, he slowly lifted Heidi to his shoulder, trying not to rouse her, all the while cupping her head protectively. He grinned at Victoria when the baby cooperated by burping audibly.

"Oops," she said. "Forgot to give you a protective cloth."

He realized then the damp warmth on his shoulder must be spit-up formula.

Later, after Heidi was asleep in the cradle, he and Victoria retired to the kitchen for lunch. He found he enjoyed helping her with the simple meal.

"I don't cook for myself," he admitted as they sat down to eat.

"No food to speak of in your refrigerator at the town house gave me that clue," she said. "But you're not alone. Many single people don't like to cook for themselves, especially men."

"I'm not home all that much."

"Your job requires travel?"

He nodded without elaborating.

Victoria didn't pry any further. Steve had taken her injury in stride, not saying a word about her downright stupidity in not looking where she was stepping. She was plain lucky she hadn't fallen off a cliff instead of that short drop. This was as amiable as she'd so far seen him and she didn't intend to do anything to make him retreat into his silent shell again.

"Willa Hawkins seems friendly," she offered cautiously. "I really appreciated her help."

He grunted instead of replying. So much for that. Victoria wondered what he'd say if she told him Willa called him the secret man. Probably another grunt.

They ate in silence until he suddenly said, "Tell me about Kim. I know you said some things about her and the accident when we first met in the hospital but I wasn't really listening. Start from the beginning, will you?"

Victoria began with the ambulance bringing in Kim as an accident victim. "She had multiple injuries and we might have transferred her to Washington Hospital Center for specialized trauma care but as soon as we saw she was in advanced labor that wasn't an option. The baby was on the way and needed to be delivered then and there."

She went on relating in layman terms what had happened, avoiding too-realistic descriptions. "So after Kim had signed the papers, she closed her eyes and I knew she was going. I was still holding her hand and she mumbled your name and then something I couldn't quite catch, even though I leaned close to hear."

"What do you think she said?" The tenseness in Steve's voice troubled Victoria, making her wish she had something comfortably concrete to tell him.

"What it sounded like was 'unfair day' and then 'cold.' These are only the approximate words, her voice was pretty indistinct by then."

She saw by his puzzled expression that he could make no more sense of the words than she had. Of course it certainly had been an unfair day for Kim and she may well have felt cold.

"Nothing else?" he asked.

Victoria shook her head. "I know how you must feel."

His gaze held hers. "I doubt that. The truth is, there was no chance Kim and I would ever get together again and we both knew it. Her death was a shock but not the kind of shock it would have been if we'd still been close."

She stared into his hazel eyes, gone hard and cold, and tried to determine what he might be hiding behind that icy gaze. Denial?

"I should have mentioned it before," he added, "but I didn't realize you'd be with me this long."

"I didn't, either," she said. "What I'm wondering is if the reason you told me about you and Kim is because it bothers you to accept sympathy."

He blinked. "Blunt to a fault, aren't you? Let's say I don't care to accept anything under false pretenses."

"So you're asking me to withdraw my sympathy?"

"Yes."

Victoria shrugged and immediately regretted it when pain settled into her left shoulder. Damn, this injury was going to be a bother. As for sympathy, if he didn't want it, she wouldn't waste any more on him.

"Shoulder bothering you?" he asked.

The man didn't miss much. "Now and then."

"When you need help, ask." He offered a half smile. "I have unexplored talents."

She decided she'd be better off not asking about them.

Throughout the rest of the day and evening, he assisted her with Heidi and with household tasks unasked. It wasn't until she was ready to go to bed that she realized there was no way she was going to get her T-shirt off without causing herself more pain than she wanted to experience. The alternative—to leave it on—wasn't viable. Sooner or later the shirt had to come off.

Steve was sprawled on the couch in the main room reading by the light of a kerosene lamp. He put down the book and looked up when Victoria said, "Excuse me."

She stood beside the couch looking distressed.

"What's wrong?" he asked, sitting up.

"My arm—that is, I'm going to need some help with this shirt."

Rising, he assessed the situation, resolved to treat it with detachment. "The shirt will have to come off the injured arm last," he said.

"I realize that." Her tone was tart.

Was she embarrassed about him seeing her brassiere? He tried to keep from wondering if it was one of those lacy confections that showed as much as it concealed. This was no time to let his imagination run riot. Especially since he'd probably have to unhook it for her. Would it have a back or a front closure? His groin tightened.

"Let's get this over with," he said gruffly and reached for the bottom of her T-shirt.

She backed away. "Uh—could you do it with your eyes closed?"

"If I have to." He tried not to show his amusement. "Let me take hold of the shirt first."

"I wish I could be more practical about this," she muttered. "After all, it has nothing to do with sex."

From his point of view she was about as wrong as she could be. "Here goes," he said, grasping the shirt bottom with both hands and easing it up, belatedly remembering to close his eyes—so belatedly that he caught a glimpse of one bare breast. She wasn't wearing a brassiere.

"Careful," she warned.

Much too late, as far as he was concerned, though he did his best to control his instinctive reaction.

With his eyes still closed, he let her movements guide the way he pulled the shirt. When at last she said, "Okay, you can let go now," he obeyed.

As his hands dropped away from her, his fingertips accidentally grazed a soft swelling that he knew was one of her breasts. Fighting an impulse to open his eyes, he swallowed and turned away.

"Let's hope you heal quickly," he said hoarsely.

Shaken by Steve's touch, Victoria hurried into the bedroom. The entire disrobing had been too distractingly intimate to ever be repeated. Painful shoulder or not, she'd manage to dress and undress herself from now on.

Heidi's hungry wail roused her at three in the morning. Steve, too, obviously, because he came barreling down the spiral staircase as she bent over the cradle. He was, she noted absently, still wearing the same seen-better-days pajama bottoms.

"I'll change her," he announced. "You warm the formula."

After Steve fed and burped the baby, she whimpered when he tried to put her back in the cradle. "Now what?" he asked.

"She isn't ready to go back to sleep."

"I am," he grumbled. But despite his gruff words, he sat down in the rocker again, still holding the baby, and set it in motion.

Amused and touched, Victoria said, "Know any lullabies?"

To her surprise, he began humming a plaintive, singsong tune. "Talal's," he said. "He sings it to Yasmin in Arabic. Something about the cool desert breeze bringing the gift of sleep."

This was the first time Steve had voluntarily offered anything at all about his personal life. She would have liked to ask who Talal and Yasmin were but didn't want to break the spell cast by the intimate coziness of the night, dark except for the beams of their two flashlights crossing each other as they rested side by side on the kitchen table.

Whatever the song was, Heidi quieted, seeming to like Steve's humming as he rocked back and forth.

"At camp," Victoria said softly, "I remember waiting for sleep while listening to the wind sighing through the pines. One moment we'd all be chattering and then one by one my cabin mates would fall asleep. I was always the last, I guess because I wanted to savor every moment."

She went on reminiscing until she realized the creak of the rocker had ceased. Peering closely at Steve, she saw he was sleeping as soundly as the baby in his arms.

Much as she hated to disturb him, she knew that,

relaxed as he was, if he moved in his sleep Heidi might roll off his lap.

Rising from her chair, she leaned over the rocker, careful not to touch him. Experience had taught her some sleepers reacted violently to being touched. "Steve," she whispered. "Steve, you need to wake up."

To her shock, he bounded out of the chair, only his last-minute instinctive grab saving the baby from a fall. Heidi let out an indignant wail.

"It's all right," he said to the baby, cuddling her to him. "I'd never do anything to hurt you."

"I didn't mean to startle you," Victoria told him. "You certainly have a hair-trigger reaction time."

"Something like that, yeah."

"Heidi likes to be rocked. Maybe if you put her in the cradle we can rock her to sleep in that."

When he did as she suggested, she thought he might let her take over and go back to bed. Instead, he began swinging the cradle gently back and forth, once again humming the Arabic lullaby. When Heidi slipped back into sleep he mouthed a silent good-night and headed for the stairs.

Once in her own bed, despite an occasional twinge from her shoulder, Victoria dozed off feeling a warm glow of accomplishment. Maybe her fall hadn't been so foolish after all since, as a result, Steve had begun to act like a father.

The next morning she was amazed to see how late it was when she woke. Bounding out of bed, she checked the cradle. Heidi lay in it happily waving her arms.

"She's been fed and changed," Steve said from the kitchen area.

"Did she cry? I didn't hear her."

"I was already up when she began to whimper so I took care of things." He held up the pot. "Coffee's ready. Need any help dressing?"

Belatedly conscious of her short sleep-T, she began to retreat. "I think I can manage," she told him firmly, determined to do so or die trying.

Underpants and shorts were fairly easy to manage. A bra was impossible, but then she often went without one. As she'd been forced to reveal to Steve last night, to her dismay. Keeping in mind she needed to be able to remove all her clothes by herself tonight, she chose a shirt that buttoned up the front, though fastening the buttons one-handedly proved to be a struggle. Her shoulder was definitely improving, though.

Steve watched Victoria emerge from the bedroom fully dressed and told himself it was just as well he didn't have to get involved in that again. So far, taking care of the baby had proved to be a breeze, but taking care of the baby's caretaker could start up a storm.

He caught himself admiring the graceful curves of her legs revealed by the shorts, and deliberately looked away.

"After breakfast we'll give Heidi a bath," Victoria said, "so let's put some water on the stove to warm now."

"There's already warm water in the reservoir." Seeing her puzzled expression, he added, "It's at the far end of the stove, away from the fire." As he spoke, he walked over and, with the metal lifter, opened the hinged lid of the reservoir.

Victoria peered in and poked a cautious finger at the water. "Great. Plenty here to use for the baby. Now if only we could find a way to get a warm shower for grown-ups out of this."

"I'm hunting for a wood-fired hot-water tank for the bathroom. I know they're made but haven't had time to locate one."

"Ah, well, cold showers are supposed to be good for mind and body according to some health freak."

Deciding it wouldn't improve his health any to imagine her in the shower—warm or cold—he changed the subject. "When your shoulder's better we'll pack up Heidi and hike down the trail to Hanksville, the little community I told you about on this side of the mountain. Tiny place. One general store, a post office, gas station, a few houses and a church."

"Maybe the day after tomorrow? I'm healing rapidly, just as you hoped."

After breakfast, Victoria perched the plastic baby tub she'd bought on the kitchen table and Steve filled it with a bucket of water from the reservoir. Once he was convinced the wet baby wouldn't slip out of his grasp, the bath went well.

"Old Steve didn't drown you, after all," he told Heidi as he patted her dry. "Might be a tad clumsy but I'm a fast learner."

Her tiny lips curved up and, pleased, he turned to tell Victoria, "She's smiling at me."

"More likely to be gas. It takes about three to six weeks for babies to work up to smiling on purpose."

"Don't listen to her," he told the baby. "We know what we know."

Victoria rolled her eyes. "I won't say another word."

At some level, Steve was aware it was ridiculous to be talking to Heidi as though she was already a rational person, but at another, basic level, he enjoyed doing it. No one could have convinced him of this a couple weeks ago, but there it was.

He'd undergone some metamorphosis from being more or less indifferent to the baby into becoming Heidi's protector. She needed him in a way no human being ever had. "Old Steve'll take good care of you," he murmured while fastening the tabs of her diaper. "He won't let anything hurt you."

Glancing up, he saw Victoria's grin of approval and shrugged. So he was acting like the protective father he wasn't. But it was no act. He'd begun to care what happened to this little girl. And, somehow, mixed up in the process was the realization he also cared what Victoria thought about him. When he shouldn't give a damn.

Later in the morning she persuaded him to don what he thought of as the kangaroo pouch and, with Heidi in it, they took a short walk outside.

After lunch, with the baby asleep in the cradle, he decided to split some more firewood.

Victoria was alone in the house with the baby when the front door opened a crack and a woman's voice called, "Yoo-hoo, anyone home?" Willa Hawkins's wrinkled brown face poked around the edge of the door.

"Come in, please do," Victoria said.

"How're you doing, gal?" Willa asked, ambling over with her lidded wicker basket to peer into the cradle. "Cute little punkin." She crossed to a chair near Victoria and sat down with the basket on her lap. "Told you I'd be over to check and here I am."

"My shoulder's better. I'm so grateful you were there to help me."

"Healthy young gal like you should heal up right quick. Getting along with the secret man, are you?"

"My sore shoulder is forcing him to be a bit more outgoing. He's actually learned to take care of his daughter."

"Not up to taking care of you yet, though, I'd say. Going to take him a while. Got to be patient with men like him."

Hoping Willa didn't mean what it sounded like she meant, Victoria said somewhat stiffly, "We have an employer-employee relationship."

"My eye. Any time a fine, healthy male and a pretty little gal get together, there's bound to be more 'n that. Take your time. No need to rush. Better for the waiting, most always."

"Willa, there's nothing like that between us." Victoria firmly changed the subject. "Can I get you some lemonade?"

"I'd like that. The babe's got red hair, like you."

"Steve's wife had red hair."

"Yeah, I know she's not yours. Could be, though."

Pouring lemonade from the pitcher into two glasses, Victoria was taken aback at her sudden surge of possessiveness triggered by Willa's words. *She wanted Heidi to be hers.*

Impossible! But the impossibility didn't defuse her yearning.

A yowl from inside Willa's basket made her turn and look at the old woman.

"Bevins says it's time to get out," Willa remarked, opening the lid.

A black-and-gray-striped kitten climbed from the basket onto Willa's lap, then leapt to the floor. Tail up, he sauntered into the kitchen and sniffed cautiously at Victoria's ankle before rubbing against her leg.

"Oh, my," she said, reaching down to pick him up. "I didn't realize the kitten was in your basket."

As Bevins climbed onto her shoulder to survey his new surroundings, the back door opened and Steve walked in.

"What in blue blazes is that cat doing in here?" he demanded.

Chapter Five

In the cabin's main room, Willa stood up and faced Steve. "Bevins is here to rid you of the mice, Mr. Henderson. Not to harm your daughter."

Steve stared from her to Victoria and back. "Bevins?"

"A banker I knew years ago wore a striped gray suit much like the kitten's coat," Willa said. "His name was Bevins."

Steve waved a dismissive hand. "You can't bring a cat near a baby."

Willa met his angry glare with calmness. "Why ever not?"

"Babies are helpless. Can't protect themselves against being scratched or bitten. Or worse. It might get on her chest and suffocate her."

"He, not it, Mr. Henderson. And cats don't suffocate babies. Victoria'll second my telling you cats sucking a baby's breath is old wives' superstition. As for the rest, 'twould be simple to teach Bevins the cradle is off-limits, but I've changed my mind about leaving the poor critter with an ignorant man like you.'' Willa headed for Victoria who was still holding the kitten.

Bevins leapt off Victoria's shoulder onto the kitchen table, down to a chair, then the floor and streaked across the room and through the shed between the main room and the back door, left ajar by Steve.

Willa fixed Steve with a stern gaze. "'Tis clear the kit wants to stay, so 'twill be up to you to bring him back to me.'' She nodded to Victoria, turned her back on Steve, marched to the front door, opened it and was gone.

"Interfering old woman," Steve muttered.

Watching him, Victoria said, "She's right about one thing—cats don't suck anyone's breath.''

"Never said they did. But I still don't like the idea of a cat in the same house with the baby.''

"Actually, he isn't. He's outside the house. And he's only a baby himself, too young to be out there with no protection from wild animals.''

"With any luck he'll follow Willa home.''

Victoria raised her eyebrows. "Unlikely.''

"Damn it. I refuse to be made to feel guilty about that kitten. I didn't ask for him.'' As Steve spoke, it occurred to him he hadn't asked for Heidi, either. Somehow fate had chosen to inundate him with helpless little creatures.

He wouldn't admit it to Victoria, but he knew he'd

have to find the kitten—Bevins, what a ridiculous name, sounded like a butler—before nightfall or he'd worry about its safety.

"I've been thinking about getting a dog while we're here," he said abruptly. "Wouldn't hurt to have a watchdog around."

"What about when we leave? Do they allow pets in your town house complex?"

He shook his head. They didn't. He hadn't gotten that far along in his planning. He was confident no one could learn where he was but the idea of a dog had come to him when he'd held Heidi to feed her. He was determined to keep her safe. Dogs were extra protection, just in case. With a dog tied outside, he'd have fair warning of any intruders, if the worst should happen. Not that he expected it to.

"I could take Bevins when we leave here," Victoria said, "but there's a no-dog rule at my apartment complex."

"We haven't yet found Bevins," he reminded her. "As far as the dog goes, it'd serve Willa right if we gave it to her as a farewell present. A dog in exchange for the cat."

She smiled slightly. "So we're keeping the kitten after all?"

He wasn't thrilled about it. "Do you honestly think he won't harm Heidi?"

"Kittens and babies have existed together for centuries. In my entire career as a nurse I never saw any infant injured by a cat. Children, yes, because they interact with cats and tend to get scratched—usually not seriously. But I'll certainly watch out for her safety."

He nodded, convinced she would. He'd watched Victoria with the baby. She treated Heidi with more than merely good nursing care; he detected a loving fondness. Almost as though she were the baby's mother. Which she wasn't—any more than he was Heidi's father.

He left the cabin to search for Bevins but found no trace of the kitten. Victoria asked about putting scraps of meat out to attract him but he vetoed that, telling her food left outside was likely to attract a bear.

Darkness came without them locating the kitten. Steve tried to convince himself and Victoria that Bevins had, after all, followed Willa home. Or maybe the mother cat had come looking for him and led him back there.

"I hope you're right," she said dubiously.

As he gave Heidi her evening bottle, he marveled at how she cuddled into him as he held her, her blue eyes examining him gravely as he fed her.

Yes, he'd get a dog, even though they were safe enough here. He wasn't a man to be careless of details, but he might have overlooked something. A dog would be an extra security measure.

The next morning, after helping Victoria with the baby, he waited until Heidi settled down for a nap before saying, "I'm driving into Aylestown. Anything you need?"

"Milk and fresh fruit," she said. "Also, we have to find a Laundromat soon. There's a limit to how much I can hand wash."

"Next time," he promised.

After another sortie into the woods around the

cabin failed to turn up the kitten, he drove down the steep, winding road, thinking about how easy it was to have Victoria around. She wasn't afraid of stating her opinion, often opposite to his, but she didn't start foolish arguments. Or flounce off in a snit. In short, she was about as unlike Kim as she could be. If only he wasn't so damned attracted to her—a complication he hadn't figured in—their time up here in the mountains could be restful and relaxing.

In Aylestown, he made a phone call to the agency, telling them he was passing through on his way north because he was aware they'd pinpoint where he was calling from. He was on leave, they didn't need to know his every move.

There was nothing new on Malengo. He hung up and asked the store clerk if there was a nearby animal shelter.

"Nope. Nearest one's at the county seat," the man said. "You lose a dog, mister?"

"Why?"

"On account of we got a stray hanging around here. No collar, don't belong to nobody in town, must've been left here by some tourist. You, maybe?"

Steve shook his head.

The man shrugged. "Too bad. Ain't nobody willing to take him in. We all got enough dogs of our own. Sure you don't want him? He's healthy enough."

Why not? Steve asked himself. It would avoid having to drive the miles to the county seat plus having to give a false name and address at the animal shelter.

"Where is he?"

"Out in back somewheres."

Behind the store, Steve viewed the multicolored medium-size dog with a critical eye. Strange-looking beast—pure mongrel. "Yo," he said to the animal, holding out his hand.

The dog cocked his head, hesitated, then walked slowly toward him and sniffed at his fingers.

"Want to go with me?" Steve asked.

The mutt wagged his tail.

"Come on, then."

Without hesitation the dog followed him to the van and leapt inside when he opened the door. When he stopped for groceries and canine supplies, the dog stayed inside. As Steve emerged, he watched a couple of teenagers on in-line skates stop by the van. The dog growled at them and they took off.

"Good boy," he told the mutt, patting its head as he climbed into the van. If the dog was already protecting the van, he'd accepted the responsibility of looking out for his new master's property. Weird-colored mongrel or not, this animal was exactly what he needed.

When they got back to the cabin, Victoria took one look at Steve's new acquisition and began to laugh. The dog promptly licked her hand.

"So he's a mutt," Steve said.

"He looks so comical with that spot of black over one eye and the yellow one over the other. It's as though a committee put him together for a joke."

"He needs a name."

She fondled the dog's ears, one of which stood up while the other lay down. "How about Joker?"

Steve smiled. "Perfect."

He fed Joker, put a new collar on him, then rigged up a post and tied the dog in back of the cabin. He and Victoria were eating supper when they heard scratching at the rear door. Steve frowned.

"That dog shouldn't be able to reach the door," he muttered, getting up.

Victoria watched him stride over and fling open the door. In trotted Joker, a rope trailing from his new collar. In his mouth he carried something. She drew in her breath as she recognized the limp form of the kitten. Was the poor thing dead? she wondered. Swerving around Steve, who was trying to grab the rope, Joker made a beeline for Victoria, laid the kitten in her lap, sat down and looked expectantly at her.

Very much alive, Bevins shook himself, hissed at the dog and climbed onto Victoria's shoulder.

"You don't look like a retriever," she told Joker, patting him, "but I guess you must be."

Grinning, she glanced at Steve who was shaking his head. When he caught her eye, they both began to laugh.

"All we need now," he said finally, "is a bowl of goldfish."

She knew he meant to complete the picture of the ideal family—mother, father, child, cat, dog—and goldfish. Instead of being amused, though, the thought sobered her. Not only were they not a family, but the baby wasn't hers. And neither was Steve. Not that she wanted him.

"Maybe we should let Willa know Bevins is okay," she said.

"She'll find out soon enough."

Victoria blinked, "What do you mean?"

"You didn't think she left us alone for good, did you? She'll be back." His tone was resigned.

"I like her," Victoria said defiantly. "I don't see why you're so unfriendly."

He shrugged. "Wait'll you see her other pets."

"What pets?"

He didn't answer, reaching for Joker's rope. The dog forestalled him by scooting sideways, then padding over to the cradle where he peered in at the sleeping baby, sniffing carefully. He then lay down beside the cradle, put his head on his paws and closed his eyes.

"You certainly got yourself a guard dog," she told Steve.

Two days later, Willa returned, as Steve had predicted. By now, if she was careful, Victoria could use her arm quite normally and had resumed taking care of Heidi. When Willa came inside the cabin, Victoria was just putting the baby down for a nap. Bevins was already asleep atop a cushion on the raised hearth. Steve was somewhere outside.

"See the mister got himself a dog," Willa said. "Critter growled at me till he got told I was a friend." She smiled slightly. "Figured the mister didn't much like lying to the dog."

Victoria couldn't help smiling back, though she did try to compensate by saying, "Steve has hermit tendencies."

"Got 'em myself," Willa said. "Wouldn't be living on top of a mountain otherwise." She eyed the sleeping kitten. "How's he working out?"

"He's formed a truce with Joker—that's the dog—

and with Steve, but I don't think he's chased any mice." She went on to tell how Joker had found the kitten and brought it to them.

Willa nodded. "So your only problem now is the mister."

Victoria started to deny this, then thought better of it. Willa went her own way no matter what anyone said.

"Trouble is, the man's unhappy," the old woman went on. "Not from grief, no. It comes from deep down, from the spirit. I suspect he never learned to be happy. Must be why you're here—to teach him."

Victoria shook her head. "I'm here for the baby."

"She don't take all your time."

"No, but that's my job—caring for her." Victoria rose, eager to switch to another subject. "I'll make some tea."

"Tea'd be nice. Be nice if you got over your own problem, too. Men are men but some ain't so bad's others. Don't do no good to compare one to another."

Victoria was provoked into saying, "I'm not!"

"Good. You got to take each one as he is. Find a way to open mister up, so's you can tell if he's worth your trouble—that's my advice."

"It'd take a specialized surgical team to open that man up," Victoria muttered. Still determined to deflect Willa, she added, "I hear you have other pets besides the cats."

Willa raised her eyebrows. "Wouldn't call 'em pets, exactly. 'Tis how I make a living. Come over and visit sometime and I'll show you."

"Thanks, I'll try to do that."

"The mister had Joker a long time?" Willa asked.

"No, he just got him." Victoria told her about the dog being a stray in the town below. "He wanted a dog and Joker was conveniently available."

"Never brought a dog to his cabin before. You folks expecting trouble to follow you up here?"

Victoria laughed. "Of course not. I put it down to a new father's protectiveness. Joker must sense that 'cause it's clear he feels his job is to guard Heidi."

Willa shook her head. "With the mister closed up so tight, 'tis hard to tell."

Later, after the old woman left, her words echoed in Victoria's mind. Steve was closemouthed, no doubt about that. Not that she believed he was worried about anyone bothering them—except for Willa. He certainly did value privacy. But Victoria *would* like to learn more about him. Was he basically an unhappy man or was Willa way off base there?

That evening, with the baby settled, Joker sprawled beside the cradle and the kitten batting around a small ball of string Victoria had found in the pantry, she waited until Steve settled himself on the couch.

Not giving him time to pick up his book, she eased down beside him, taking care to leave a good space between them. "If we had the right ingredients, I'd make fudge," she said. "That's what my best friend and I used to do when we were teenagers and I spent the night with her. Her parents never cared if we messed up the kitchen."

Her plaintive tone caught Steve's attention more than her words. "I take it your parents weren't that easygoing," he said.

She sighed. "When it came to her house, my mother placed cleanliness above anything else. Since

I've gotten older, I've decided maybe it was because that's all she could control. My dad was an alcoholic.''

Despite himself, Steve's interest was piqued. He'd pigeon-holed Victoria as more together than most women. Yet she'd come from what must have been a dysfunctional family. He wondered if she'd had to grow up alone.

''Any siblings?'' he asked.

''I had a sister two years older.''

''Had?''

Victoria bit her lip. ''She disappeared when she was thirteen.''

Her distress made it evident she'd never gotten over it. ''Never found?'' he asked.

She shook her head. ''My mother didn't ever give up hope Renee would come home someday, even though the police felt the most likely scenario was that she'd been abducted and killed. My dad—'' she paused and took a deep breath. ''He got worse—so abusive, my mother finally left him. Two years ago she sent word he'd died.''

He controlled his impulse to comfort her by putting his arms around her. She might misunderstand. ''Bummer,'' he muttered. ''Compared to you, I had an ideal home life.''

Her eyes, green at this moment as the first leaves of spring, looked into his. ''You don't make it sound as though you thought it was ideal.''

Damn, she was acute. ''My dad expected perfection—that's all. He didn't accept mistakes. Made it hard to live up to his standards.''

''How about your mother?''

Somewhat to his surprise he found he wanted to tell her how his mother had died when he was small and that his father had remarried soon afterward. "My stepmother was always good to me," he went on. "No complaints there."

"Do you have any brothers or sisters?"

"One half-sister. Karen lives in Nevada." He didn't add that he sometimes envied how she'd found happiness in her growing family.

"What's she like?"

"I used to tease her by calling her Ms. Truth and Justice Prevails when she was in college. We all know life isn't fair, but that doesn't stop Karen from trying to do her best to make it as fair as she possibly can."

Victoria smiled at him. "You sound fond of her."

He was. He'd do anything for his sister and her extended family.

"I often wonder what Renee would be like now," Victoria said wistfully. "She never seemed to be afraid of our father, like I was. Or of anything, really. Her hair was redder than mine, a real carrottop, and she was feisty to go with it. Nobody ever picked on *her* little sister."

"Were her eyes that same green-gold as yours?" Steve asked, not wishing to upset her by asking questions about Renee's disappearance, which is what he really wanted to do. He might be on leave, but he found it hard to get rid of the urge to investigate anything suspicious.

"No, a sort of golden-brown. She wasn't chunky like me, either. She was tall and slim."

"I wouldn't call you chunky," he said. "More like

just right.'' He heard his own words with dismay. Watch it, Henderson, he warned himself.

To his surprise, she flushed and looked away. Without analyzing what he meant to do, he reached and put a finger under her chin, turning her face toward him again. When their eyes met, what he saw in hers made him lose his cool completely.

Wrapping his arms around her, he pulled her close, his mouth covering hers. The kiss wasn't meant to be comforting; he'd passed that point. Desire, pure and simple, drove him. He wanted her.

Before she realized what she was doing, Victoria melted into the kiss, and then it was too late to pull back. Or even want to. Whatever she'd expected from Steve wasn't this violent rush of intensifying need, of being caught up in a brilliant flare of passion she couldn't resist.

So much for sitting next to him on the couch for what she'd hoped would turn out to be a cozy chat. Willa and her damn get-him-to-open-up. What she'd done instead was to turn a tiger loose in herself as well as in him.

"Shouldn't be doing this," Steve whispered against her lips.

"Bad idea," she murmured in agreement before he captured her mouth with his again.

She was floating in a sensual haze when Bevins chose that moment to try to leap onto her lap, his tiny claws hooking into her bare leg as he fell short of his goal.

"Ouch!" Victoria pulled abruptly away from Steve, reaching to pluck the kitten from her and set him on the couch. What a painful way to be brought back to reality!

"Told you it'd be a mistake to keep that cat." The hoarseness of passion roughened Steve's voice, settling into her bones.

"Maybe it was just as well," she said.

"Yeah." He rose from the couch. "Think I'll take a stroll outside."

She could use some fresh air herself, Victoria thought. Her head certainly needed clearing—not to mention the rest of her. That kiss had been the most potent she'd ever experienced. Like a race car—zero to well over a hundred miles an hour in nothing flat.

Deciding a cold drink of water might help cool her down, she got up to get one. No more of this touchy-feely stuff if she didn't intend to get involved with him.

On the other hand, why not? It wouldn't be like making any kind of a long-term commitment. Her time here was limited. If she didn't explore this fire blazing between them, it might be something she'd always regret. True, she might also regret it if she did, but at least she'd have a few hot memories to warm her later when she'd be sleeping alone again in a cold bed.

She gulped down the water, thinking the key would be to not involve her heart, just her body. Why shouldn't two people find pleasure in one another? She no longer believed Steve was some arrogant jerk; she'd come to realize he was a pretty okay guy. A few problems, maybe, but hey, she didn't intend to live with him the rest of her life, just enjoy a short-term relationship.

It was kind of scary since she'd never before decided to do anything quite like this. And those flames *were* hot. Water or not, she still hadn't cooled down. But wasn't that all the more reason to go ahead? So she could get it out of her system?

Steve, with Joker at his side, prowled around outside the cabin in the light of the all-but-full moon.

"So much for masterful control," he told the dog. "I thought I knew myself, but it turns out I hadn't a clue. Who knew what danger lurked in the depths of those green eyes of hers?"

Joker gave a companionable little woof and Steve smiled. His father had vetoed bringing a dog into the family and, though he'd longed to have one as a child, he'd never owned a dog. Obviously he'd missed something.

"Glad you're listening, pal," he said. "Only an idiot would get involved with her, right?"

Joker whined.

After a moment, Steve said, "You may have a point. A temporary liaison wouldn't mean commitment. We won't be together in the cabin forever. Once the agency gets this mess settled, we're out of here. She goes her way, I go mine. In the meantime, though, why not take advantage of what we both want?"

He stopped and the dog paused to look up at him.

"Hey, she wanted it as much as I did. No mistaking her response." Remembering, his groin tightened.

He resumed walking. "Look at it this way. I may be an idiot but only a short-term one. What's wrong with that?"

Joker had no comment.

Chapter Six

The next few days passed with Victoria and Steve warily avoiding any physical contact. He even chose to take their dirty clothes to the Aylestown Laundromat alone rather than bringing her along. She wondered if he, like she, was both reluctant and eager to see their relationship change.

After he'd left for town and Victoria had fed and changed Heidi, she decided to tuck the baby into the pouch and walk over to Willa's. Leaving the kitten in the cabin, she brought Joker with her.

The day was sunny but a brisk breeze kept it from being too warm. The breeze also carried traces of hidden blooms perfuming the morning. Strolling along the narrow trail, under the shade of the pines and maples, with the baby making contented sounds from the pouch, Victoria felt at peace with the world. She was exactly where she wanted to be at the moment, engaged in an activity she enjoyed, along with two great, if not very talkative, companions.

"Listen to the wind in the tree branches," she murmured to Heidi. "Doesn't it sound like it's trying to whisper secrets to us?"

When she heard the raucous call of a jay, she told the baby how the bird was warning every animal within earshot of their presence. "Sort of like Joker would bark if a stranger came near," she added.

The dog, recognizing the name they'd given him, looked up at her, wagging his tail. Steve had mentioned that Joker's mere presence should be enough to discourage any dangerous wildlife from prowling around the cabin, in case she was worried about it. Actually she hadn't been.

Joker, she'd noticed, was not given to barking at every sound or unfamiliar motion, though it was clear he noticed them all. He might look bizarre, but so far he seemed to be pretty unflappable.

By the time she reached Willa's cabin, the baby was dozing, Victoria gently caressed the soft down covering Heidi's head, pushing away any thought of when she'd no longer have the right to carry this sweet weight or touch Heidi's silken skin. She'd ignore the future; today the baby was here.

She found Willa hoeing weeds in the tiny garden near her cabin, a garden enclosed with chicken wire attached to tall posts.

"Got to keep the critters out," Will said after they'd exchanged greetings. "Nothing's so enticing as forbidden fruit, be you animal or human."

Victoria reminded herself there was no way the old

woman could read her mind. In any case, Steve wasn't exactly forbidden.

Setting aside the hoe, Willa let herself out of the enclosure and led Victoria to a shedlike structure on the other side of the trail. The door was open as were the several windows and Victoria saw cages on shelves inside. She was about to step through the door when Joker, growling, blocked her entrance. At the same time she heard an ominous rattle.

Tensing, she glanced at Willa. "What's that?"

"No need to fash yourself, I keep my snakes shut safely away." She shooed Joker away from the entrance, saying to him, "They can't hurt Victoria or the baby."

Victoria made no move to go inside. "Rattlesnakes?"

"What the mister calls my pets. 'Tis true I take good care of them so they'll stay healthy enough to support me. When I need funds or when I get a request from laboratories, I milk them of their venom and ship it off. 'Tis worth a pretty penny."

Peering in through the open door, Victoria could see maybe half a dozen cages containing snakes. She had no desire to go any closer. "Isn't that dangerous?" she asked Willa.

"Some. Got bit a time or two before I learned to be more than careful."

"Good grief! It's a wonder you survived."

"I may be old but I ain't foolish. Put by some of that antivenin those laboratories make, just in case. Came in mighty handy."

"Where did you get the snakes?"

"Collected 'em myself," Willa said proudly.

Victoria shuddered. "I'm impressed. Handling snakes is something I could never do."

Joker, who hadn't left her side, seemed as relieved as Victoria when they turned away from the shed. He bounded ahead, tail wagging.

"So you see 'tis the mister's little joke, calling those rattlers my pets," Willa said, "when 'tis nothing more than an old lady's way to keep afloat."

"I don't think it's a kind joke," Victoria said, angry with Steve.

Willa shrugged. "Any man who makes his peace with a cat he didn't want in the first place has a good heart. Might be buried deep within, but 'tis there."

Into Victoria's mind flashed the image of Bevins sleeping on Steve's knee last evening while he read his book. "The darn cat seems to prefer him to me now," she admitted as they reached the cabin.

Willa smiled. "'Tis the way of cats to know who they need to charm. Come inside and take some tea with me."

Later, walking back to Steve's cabin, Victoria decided Willa was one of the most interesting women she'd ever met. A tad eccentric, maybe, but fascinating to talk to. A shame Willa lived in such an isolated spot because, once Victoria returned home, she'd probably never see the old woman again. Not that she always understood Willa's cryptic remarks—like her parting words.

"Some of the most beautiful flowers blossom only in the full of the moon," Willa had told her. "'Tis worth remembering."

Which made little sense. At the moment anyway.

Victoria hoped Steve wouldn't mind too much that

she'd invited Willa to come for lunch two days from now. True, it was his cabin and, technically, she was his employee, but their relationship had advanced beyond that. Or at least she thought it had.

To be truthful, she wouldn't object if it kept on advancing. At the moment, though, they seemed to be in stasis.

Heidi woke up and began to fuss, concentrating Victoria's attention on her. She began to sing nonsense songs to the baby, songs she hadn't recalled since her camp days and was surprised she still could remember. Must be the magic in the mountain air.

Steve tried to quash his stab of alarm when he found the cabin deserted except for Bevins. Joker was nowhere in sight so obviously the three of them were out for a stroll. But why hadn't Victoria thought to leave a note?

Because she believed she'd be back before you, he told himself firmly. Nothing's wrong.

The kitten began to climb up his pant leg and he reached down to collect it, absently petting Bevins as he peered first from the back door and then from the front.

"You must know where they went," he said to the cat as they stood in the doorway. "Too bad you can't talk."

It didn't help his increasing uneasiness to tell himself he'd gotten home sooner than she would have expected. Where were they?

Finally deciding Victoria might have taken the baby to Willa's, he shut Bevins in the cabin and started down the trail. He hadn't gone more than ten feet before he heard singing. Something that made no sense about them all rolling over and one falling out.

"Victoria?" he called, breaking into a run.

"Steve?" she answered.

He rounded a twist in the trail and saw Joker bounding toward him. Victoria, with Heidi in the pouch, was behind the dog, her face alight with greeting. He'd never seen a more welcome sight.

Instead of saying so, he snapped, "Next time you take off without warning, have the sense to leave me a note."

For a moment, as her pace slowed, she looked as though he'd struck her. He was cursing himself when her chin came up and she met his gaze levelly.

"I'm sorry," she said in a voice that would freeze water. "I didn't expect you back so soon."

Exactly as he'd told himself.

Unable to apologize or to try to explain that his scare had made him unreasonable, he turned on his heel and marched back to the cabin. Joker, who'd been by his side, abandoned him, heading back along the trail to join Victoria again.

Steve decided it was time to split more wood. Exercise might banish what his sister used to call the evil imp sitting on his left shoulder. Next time he went into town he'd have to call Karen, just to touch base.

As he stripped off his shirt and picked up the ax, he wondered why it was so hard for him to admit he was wrong. It'd been that way as far back as he could remember. Not that he was often wrong these days. But he had been just now, no doubt about that.

Victoria heard the *chink-chunk* of the ax before she

reached the front door. Good. She wouldn't have to face him for a while. If they weren't on top of a mountain, she'd be tempted to walk out and not look back. Except she couldn't abandon Heidi, not under any circumstances.

In a way, it was like Kim had given the baby to her to care for. A fanciful thought, but one she couldn't shake. Would Kim have wanted her to take care of Steve, as well? Victoria shook her head. Now that was being just plain ridiculous!

Whatever had made her believe she wanted to make love with him? Willa could say he had a good heart all she wanted to, but, if he did, it was buried too deep to ever be found.

Heidi was crying in earnest by the time she entered the cabin, and Victoria lifted the baby from the pouch. Heidi was wet and probably hungry. And maybe affected by Victoria's own angry tenseness. Infants could be incredibly sensitive to the emotions of their caretakers.

Victoria tried to stow away her annoyance with Steve as she changed the baby, but it simmered close to the surface. It wasn't what he'd said, but how he'd said it. Had he spoken politely, asking her to please leave a note if she planned to be out, she would have agreed without rancor and there'd be no problem.

Willa had insisted he was unhappy. Maybe so, but did that give him the right to try to make everyone around him as unhappy as he was? She was certainly glad she hadn't gone ahead and furthered their relationship by word or deed. They were now back to square one and, if she had anything to do with it, here they'd stay.

Once she had the baby quietly settled into the cradle Victoria began sorting and putting away the clean clothes he'd brought back from the Laundromat. That was another thing. He hadn't asked her if she wanted to go into town with him; he'd just assumed she didn't. No matter that he'd been right—she'd enjoyed visiting with Willa instead—he should have asked.

By the time he finally ventured through the back door, she'd abandoned her initial plan of treating him with chill silence in favor of blunt confrontation.

"Why must you be so ill-mannered?" she demanded. "I'm a person, not a thing. Treat me like one!"

Steve blinked. "I expect to be told where you are. What's ill-mannered about that?"

"The way you behave toward me. Like I don't deserve common courtesy."

He frowned. "You mean I forgot to say 'please.'"

"Among other things, yes. If you'd asked me to go into town with you in the first place, none of this would have happened." Gripped by what she'd decided was righteous anger, Victoria was dimly aware she wasn't quite making sense, but couldn't stop the words from pouring out.

"Assumptions!" she cried. "You're always making assumptions. You never ask me what I'd like to do. Why?"

His confused expression goaded her on.

"How could you kiss me that way when I don't matter to you in the slightest? When I mean no more than—than—" To her horror, her voice broke and tears filled her eyes. She turned from him, heading for the privacy of her bedroom, refusing to give him the satisfaction of seeing her cry.

As she passed the cradle, Heidi began to wail. Victoria paused.

"Never mind. I'll see to her," Steve said.

Victoria wanted to tell him to stuff it, but she had enough sense left to realize she might well upset the baby more if she tended to her right now. Unable to trust her voice enough to answer, she hurried inside her room, shut the door and flung herself onto the bed, sobbing.

Damn men, anyway, especially this insensitive clod she was isolated on the top of a mountain with.

The storm of tears didn't last long. Victoria had learned as a child that crying was not a solution to any problem. She sat up, wiped her face with tissues and crossed the room to look at herself in the oak-framed mirror over the dresser. Not as bad as she'd expected.

When Victoria and her sister were little and had been whacked by their father for some real or imagined infraction, Renee used to get mad at her after they stopped crying. While her sister's face would turn blotchy and her eyes red from crying, Victoria got by with no more than a pink nose from blowing it. Renee had always claimed that wasn't fair.

Victoria sighed, sending up a little prayer that Renee was safe and happy wherever she might be before carefully putting away the memory of her sister. She ran a brush through her hair and opened the door to her room.

Steve sat in the rocker feeding Heidi. Evidently he hadn't heard her door open because he was looking down at the baby with what she recognized as the besotted gaze of a new father. As she stood watching, what remained of her anger melted away like snow in August. He did have some redeeming qualities, after all.

Eventually he glanced up, saw Victoria and his expression shifted into neutral.

"She's taken to you," Victoria said.

"Probably because I know what I'm doing now—thanks to a persistent teacher." He half smiled. "As well as a good one."

She took that to mean he wanted a truce. Well, so did she. Not that she meant to back down.

"Too bad my teacher isn't able to do as thorough a job instructing me in common courtesy," he added. "I'm not always a good student."

Which was as close as she'd ever get to an apology, she supposed. But it was one, of sorts, and she gave him a wary smile. The kitten rubbed against her ankle, mewing, and she picked him up.

Steve transferred Heidi up against his shoulder, patting her back. "Bevins tried to join us, but I convinced him feeding time was off-limits. Never before realized cats sulked. When I was a kid, we didn't have pets at home."

She remembered him telling her how his father had always demanded perfection. No wonder there were no pets; animals fell far short of perfect.

"I couldn't have a pet when I was little, either," she said without thinking. "It wasn't safe. Not after my father kicked my sister's puppy when he was drunk and killed the poor little thing. I don't suppose he meant to, but…" Her voice trailed off.

Enough of the past. Petting Bevins, she said, "You mentioned something about a foot trail to a little hamlet—Hanksville?—on the other side of the mountain from Aylestown. Could we all hike down there soon?"

Steve nodded. "I remember promising you we'd do just that. How about the day after tomorrow?"

"Um, could we make it the day after that? I invited Willa for lunch two days from now."

Heidi rewarded him with a burp and he settled her back down and offered her the bottle again. "No problem," he said, somewhat to Victoria's surprise.

"I like to be neighborly," she said, somewhat defiantly, well aware he didn't feel the same, particularly.

Steve didn't intend to touch that one. "What did you think of Willa's pets?" he asked.

"I wouldn't call them pets. Those snakes are her living."

"She's braver than I am," he admitted. Grinning, he added, "And even more oddball."

Victoria shot him a challenging look. "About even-steven, from where I stand."

"Thought I'd grill steaks outside tonight," he said, changing the subject before he got skewered. "Picked some up in town, along with a small grill and some charcoal."

"Sounds divine—but can we? You're so careful about leaving no food outside because of the possibility of attracting bears."

"Have to do a thorough clean-up job afterward, that's all. Besides, we now have Joker for an early-warning system."

Steve turned out to have a mean touch with charcoal. The steaks were done to absolute perfection and went well with the potatoes she'd baked in the woodstove's oven—her first venture into using it. Topped off with a fresh fruit salad, the meal was delicious.

"You can cook for me anytime," she told him afterward.

"I'll keep it in mind." His words were light but the look in his changeable hazel eyes as well as what he said next made her catch her breath.

"Full moon tonight."

Willa's words sprang into her head and came out of her mouth. "The most beautiful flowers blossom then."

His slow smile set her pulses racing. "We'll have to discover what they are, won't we?"

She didn't answer, couldn't answer, unsure of what she wanted to say as well as unsure of what she wanted. Where he was concerned her emotions seemed to flip-flop with maddening regularity, either all systems go or a complete shutdown—never on neutral.

Taking her time getting ready for the night, she tried to decide whether it was wise to venture outside with Steve under a full moon—or not. Once the baby was soundly asleep, though, and Steve took her hand, leading her toward the door, she discovered that wisdom had nothing to do with her decision.

On the way to the door he plucked Bevins from the hearth pillow and made a detour to deposit him inside the shed, shutting him in to keep him away from Heidi's cradle.

Joker, tied outside in back past the shed, whined

when he heard them leave the cabin but Steve shook his head. "Not tonight, pal," he called to the dog.

Maybe that's what I should say to Steve, Victoria told herself. But, tingling with anticipation as she was, how could she?

The moon, high overhead, shone silver light through the trees, changing the world with its night magic as they strolled along the trail leading down the mountain. Not wishing to succumb entirely to its beauty or to Steve's disturbing nearness, she said, "You really did upset me this morning."

"My sister used to say I had an evil imp that I usually kept locked up but once in a while he got out and sat on my left shoulder. He was there this morning."

"Actually, I should have left you a note."

"Please," he said softly, stopping to draw her into his arms.

Whatever the "please" was meant for, a belated politeness or a warning to say no now or it would be too late, she ignored it when his lips met hers in the sweetest of kisses. This is what she'd longed for ever since the first kiss, to feel the hard strength of his body molded to hers, to taste him again, to feel the softness of his hair under her fingers.

The scent of burning charcoal still clung to his clothes, mingling with the clean male scent of his skin. Breathing it in, she found the smell arousing because it came from him.

When she responded eagerly, he held her closer, coaxing her mouth open so he could deepen the kiss, intensifying her desire. Her thoughts fragmented into wisps and floated away. She could no longer think, but she felt his need mingling with hers until she was consumed with wanting.

His hands slid under her T-shirt and she heard him draw in a shaky breath that blended with her moan when he cupped her naked breasts. She couldn't blame it on the moonlight; this man had a magic of his own in the touch of his lips, his hands, his body.

When he pulled her shirt over her head and off, she reached for his, needing to feel her breasts against his naked chest and the smooth skin of his back under her hands.

"Victoria," he murmured against her lips, her name a caress.

Unable to speak coherently, she made a sound in the back of her throat similar to the kitten's purr.

Was it the moon, was it Steve, was it her own need driving her up? Or a combination of all three? Whatever made her feel so wild and abandoned didn't matter, only the sensation itself did. She couldn't get enough of him; she needed more and more.

He eased them both down under a pine, the prickly brush of pine needles teasing her bare skin as he finished undressing her. He shucked the rest of his clothes and then pulled her close again, kissing her mouth, her throat, pausing at her breasts to taste one, then the other, driving her wild.

"Steve," she managed to whisper, but no more words emerged.

His fingers found her center and she gasped with pleasure, arching under his hand. When she reached for him, she found he was completely aroused. He groaned and rose over her.

When they joined, a thrill began deep inside her,

infiltrating her entire body, infusing her with an electric passion that drove her to match his rhythm as they travelled together in their journey to a place she'd never reached before.

Afterward, as she emerged from her silvery haze, she breathed in the heady scent of their lovemaking and nodded, understanding what Willa had meant about a moon blossom.

As if reading her thought, Steve murmured, "That old gal has her act together, after all. Let's try for a bouquet."

Then he kissed her and, slowly and sensuously, they began the erotic journey all over again.

Chapter Seven

After the moonlight walk with Victoria, Steve climbed into the loft as usual. She hadn't invited him to bed down with her, nor had he expected her to. Their coming together had been inevitable, given the increasing heat between them, but he was willing to take the aftermath slow and easy, which was apparently what she wanted to do.

There should be no rush to intensify a relationship that couldn't last. Which didn't stop him from wishing he was in her bed. Their lovemaking, great as it had been, was no more than an appetizer; he was still hungry for more.

He wondered if it would have been the same back in his town house, had it been safe to remain there. Probably not. Chances were she would have insisted he find permanent help and then resumed her own life. He'd have missed this night with her; they'd never have come together in the mountain moonlight.

He hadn't ever considered himself a romantic—far from it. Yet tonight had been just that. Romantic and sexy as anything he'd ever experienced. Victoria made love like she did everything else. Thoroughly. He shifted uncomfortably. Damn, all this dwelling on how great she'd been was making him hard again.

If only life were as simple for him as it was for old Willa who stayed in her cabin year-round. At the moment, he couldn't deny living on top of this mountain had an almost irresistible appeal. Not alone, like Willa. He wanted Victoria up here with him. And Heidi. Then, of course, there was Joker and Bevins....

How had he, a loner by choice, in such a short time managed to collect not only a baby, a dog and cat, but the sexiest woman he'd ever kissed? And what was he going to do with them all when this mountain idyll ended?

Steve found he didn't want to think about the future. Not when he was having the time of his life.

Victoria told herself she was relieved when she heard Steve climb the stairs to the loft. She needed time to think about this night. On the other hand, if he'd been lying next to her, thinking is not what she'd be doing. He couldn't be compared to any other man because he was the first who'd made her feel what was between them was worth risking anything for.

Not that she expected any future with him. This episode in her life would be treasured and stored in a special memory compartment. On days when things went wrong, maybe she'd delve into that storage area and remember the silver light of the moon caressing them both with magic. She'd remember with pleasure and maybe a touch of heartache because it had to end.

Victoria shook her head. Why think about endings? Anticipate the days with Steve yet to come. And the nights…

It seemed she'd hardly been asleep when the cries of the baby woke her. Must be 3:00 a.m., she told herself as she rolled out of bed. Heidi invariably woke around then for her pre-dawn feeding.

Before she could settle into the rocker with baby and bottle, Bevins began to yowl from the shedlike attachment at the rear of the cabin where the split wood was stored. He allowed himself to be shut in there each night without complaining, but now he obviously wanted to join them.

She let him out before she sat down. He trailed her to the rocker, then tried to climb onto her lap with the baby. She pushed him off with a firm "no." Tail high, he marched to the stairs and humpty-humped up to the loft. Victoria shook her head, waiting for an explosion, but none came.

Heidi had finished half the bottle and Victoria was burping her when Steve appeared on the stairs, sleep-disheveled, with the kitten hooked over one arm. "I seem to have acquired a bed partner," he said as he came down. "Not necessarily by choice. Or the one I'd have chosen."

"You'd prefer Joker?"

He shot her a mock frown. "Very funny."

Sinking onto the couch, he set Bevins on his knee and began petting him. "Doesn't take much to get his motor revved up," he commented. "Or mine."

Glancing at him, she saw his gaze was fixed on her bare thighs, her sleep-T having ridden up when she sat in the rocker. With Heidi in her lap, she could do little about it, and an answering slow heat built in her.

"Maybe we need some rules?" She'd meant to make a statement but it came out a question.

"You think so?"

When he looked at her with his hazel eyes softened by desire, she didn't know what she thought. If anything. "I like you best with your hair all mussed up," she blurted.

He looked startled, as well he might. Whatever had possessed her to say that?

"Why?"

"I don't know—maybe it's because then your guard's down and you're not trying to be so perfect."

He was quiet for so long, she began to wonder if he'd taken what she said as an insult. Or a weakness in himself. Finally he got up from the couch, crossed to the back door and deposited Bevins in the shed again. On his return he stopped by the rocker and ran a finger over Heidi's cheek.

"So soft," he said. "Like yours." He bent and brushed her lips with his, then straightened.

"Rules?" he asked. "Do you really believe we'd follow them?"

Victoria watched him climb the stairs and disappear into the loft, realizing she understood more about Steve's body than she did his mind.

"What do you think of your father?" she whispered to Heidi. "He's that big guy who feeds and changes you sometimes, the guy who was afraid of you at first. But now he's not. Now he loves you."

She cuddled the baby to her, not saying the words in her heart. She loved Heidi, too.

Not Heidi's father, though. Chemistry—that's what she felt for him. Powerful chemistry. But not love.

Victoria woke late and so did Heidi. The day passed pleasantly enough, though neither of them saw much of Steve, who kept busy outside. House tasks occupied her—changing bed linen, dusting, sweeping the floor—in general neatening up the place for lunch with Willa the next day.

Though she tried not to wonder what would happen when night came, by evening every nerve was on edge. Would he? Would she? Should she? Had their intimacy been a mistake? Not in terms of how he'd made her feel, she'd never want to give that up, but a mistake because, if they grew closer, how much harder it would be to part.

As it turned out, after the evening meal, Steve helped her clean up, then sat down with his thriller and, with Bevins on his knee, began to read.

"Are thrillers the kind of book you prefer?" she asked, busy getting Heidi ready for the night.

"Busman's holiday," he said.

"What does that mean?"

He shrugged. "They're fiction, not real, so I can enjoy them."

Victoria frowned, working through that one. "You've never actually told me what you do for a living," she said finally.

"Government work. Not all that interesting."

If he didn't want to be specific, it really was none

of her business. To question him further would be prying, which she had no right to do.

She sat down in the rocker with the baby. Heidi had been fed but wasn't yet sleepy, so when Joker padded over to sniff at the baby's feet, Victoria propped her up so she could focus on the dog. Joker began wagging his tail.

"Look!" Victoria cried, alerting Steve. "She's smiling."

He put down the book, a grin lighting his face. "Yeah," he said, "but look who at. How comes it's the dog that rates her first real smile?"

That, as it turned out, was the high point of the evening. And night. Steve made no move and, since Victoria was damned if she was going to initiate anything, they went to their separate beds, having exchanged no more than a chaste good-night. She fell asleep trying to convince herself it was all for the best.

Steve got up early the next morning, bemused by the most erotic dreams he'd had in years. Dreams of Victoria. He'd had a tough time last night keeping his hands off her but, one way or another, she'd been in his bed anyway.

When he came downstairs, Heidi was just beginning to stir, making fussing noises that stopped when he lifted her from the cradle and brought her over to the makeshift changing table. She eyed him solemnly as he switched her wet diaper to a dry one.

"How come you can smile at Joker but you don't have a smile for your old—?" Steve broke off, astounded at what he'd been about to say. *Your old dad.* He wasn't. He could never be. The truth hurt because, oddly enough, he was beginning to feel like she was his daughter. How had that happened?

It made him understand why Karen had clung to infant Danny after she was left as his guardian when their cousin died. Steve had supported Karen, for a time financially as well as emotionally, not because he thought she was doing the right thing but because she was his sister and, damn it, because their folks objected to her keeping the baby.

Now his feeling for Heidi had shown him why Karen had been so adamant. Baby humans were something like puppies and kittens—take one in and you soon find you can't bear to give it up. Must be programmed into human genes.

He sat in the rocker to give Heidi the bottle and marveled at how trustingly she nestled against him. She no longer complained when, instead of Victoria, he changed or fed her—she knew him. It warmed his heart.

Apparently he did have one, despite the many times he'd been accused of being heartless. That went with his job. Which reminded him of Malengo. He and Victoria and Heidi would be hiking down to Hanksville tomorrow with Joker—he'd call the agency to see if anything was new.

How long they stayed up here at the cabin depended on how fast the agency could come up with something on Malengo. If only he'd been able to get to Kim before she died. Not only for a final farewell but because he was sure she fled from that slimy bastard after discovering something she couldn't accept.

He believed she'd have told him what it was if he'd been there.

Kim had apparently trusted Victoria, though. Why hadn't she told Victoria whatever it was she wanted to pass on to him? Actually she *had* said something odd. *Unfair day. Cold.* Which didn't make sense.

Holding the baby up to burp her, Steve let Kim's last words echo in his mind, then closed his eyes and repeated them aloud, running them together to see if they sounded any different. Intent on what he was doing, he didn't realize Victoria had come out of her bedroom and was standing beside him until she spoke.

"That's what Kim said!" she cried. "Only, you make it sound different. It sounds like *one fair day* instead of *unfair day.*"

His eyes popped open. "My God!" he exclaimed. "Oni Farraday!"

Victoria stared at him. "What's that mean?"

"It's a person. Kim gave you a person's name."

Her blank look told him she still didn't understand. Just as well she'd never heard the name before. The agency certainly knew Oni.

"Cold," he muttered. "Gold? Code?"

"You want words that sound like cold? How about coat? Colt?"

"Colt might do it. She raises horses—Arabians. But it still doesn't quite fit." He rose and handed Victoria the baby. "I've got to work this out."

By the time Willa arrived for lunch, Steve still hadn't found a solution that satisfied him. Preoccupied, he sat down at the table, letting Victoria and

Willa do the talking until Willa addressed him directly.

"I hear you got a sister in Nevada," she said. "Whereabouts?"

"Near Reno."

"How's the climate there? These mountain winters are getting to me and I figure maybe the West'd suit me."

"It's a high desert climate," he said. "Fairly dry, some snow in the winter, not much. Lots of sun."

Willa nodded. "Figure there must be rattlers, then."

"Yes, though I've never seen one."

"Sounds good for these old bones. Lots of empty space around, I'll bet, so a body wouldn't have to live cheek by jowl with others."

"Plenty of space," he assured her. "Real estate's not cheap, though."

Willa grinned. "Don't you worry none about me. Got a bit socked away, earning interest. Could swing it if I decide to. I can always go find me a few Nevada snakes if I run short."

"What would you do with the ones you have in cages here?" Victoria asked. "Turn them loose?"

"Yup. They've done well by me, earned their freedom a hundred times over. Reckon my old mama cat'll welcome more sun as much as me."

Steve decided Willa would take to Nevada just fine—she'd fit right in. "I'll ask my sister to send you some information about the area," he said.

"Got me a post office box in Hanksville, just down the mountain, number's seventy, like me."

Watching Steve scribble the number on what

looked like a business card triggered a sudden realization in Victoria. She'd forgotten about her own mail. She didn't get all that much since she used direct bank deposit plus withdrawal for bills, but by now her apartment mailbox was probably stuffed.

A good thing they were hiking down to Hanksville tomorrow, she'd pop the mailbox key in an envelope with a note to her neighbor Alice across the hall, asking her to collect the mail for the time being.

"Thank you kindly," Willa told Steve. "That's right neighborly of you."

"That's my specialty," he said, "finding other people to do the work."

"Don't hardly think so," Willa said. "You strike me as a man who doesn't trust others to do for you."

"She's got you pegged," Victoria said, laughing.

Steve shrugged. "Any idea why they named the village Hanksville?" he asked Willa.

"I figure they must've run out of Algonquin and Dutch names. I got both kinds in my background. Some of my ancestors were already here to begin with and the others got here early on. This mountain I live on—you, too, for now—was where a bunch of one set of ancestors massacred another set. Bloody times, back then."

"Long ago," Victoria said.

Willa nodded. "'Cept I got an uneasy feeling something's brewing." She eyed Steve assessingly. "You know anything about that?"

He shook his head. "Safe as being in your mother's arms up here nowadays."

"Could be we're just in for some bad weather,"

Willa conceded. ''One trouble with hunches—you never can pin 'em down for sure.''

Victoria, who'd never had a hunch, smiled at her and said, ''I don't think I've ever felt so safe in my entire life.''

After Willa left, Steve helped Victoria clean up, surprising her. He'd done the same last night. Maybe he'd just gotten into the habit because he'd had to give her a hand after she'd hurt her shoulder. Whatever the reason, she appreciated it.

''Good lunch,'' he said. ''Willa's a sharp old bird. Talk about pegging—I had her all wrong. I can see why you like her. Don't often make a mistake about people, but I did with her.''

''Maybe it's 'cause you got into the habit of keeping to yourself since you and Kim separated.''

''Most hermits are born, not made, my clever little analyst. I've never been Mr. Gregarious.''

She tried to picture Steve working a party like Jordan used to, slapping men on the shoulder, telling jokes, hugging women and flirting with them. Impossible! She began to giggle.

''What's so funny?''

She tried to tell him, but couldn't stop laughing. ''Thank heaven you're not like Jordan the Jerk,'' she finally managed to say.

''Who's he?''

''A doctor I used to know.''

''He move away? Get sick and die?''

Victoria hit him on the arm. ''You know what I mean.''

''Not really.'' He took her hand and led her past

Heidi, sleeping in the cradle, and out the front door to where the two Adirondack chairs angled toward one another. "Sit down and tell me why I'm not like Jordan the Jerk and why you don't know him anymore."

From the spruce behind her chair, a chickadee warbled its distinctive notes. A cool breeze sifted through the branches of the pines alongside the cabin, diluting the sun's warmth to just right. No one could ask for a more perfect afternoon. Joker came around from the back, trailing his rope again, and put his head on Steve's knee.

"Escape artist," Steve muttered, scratching him behind the ears before fixing his attention on Victoria again. "Well?"

She'd come to a decision. "I won't say a word unless we swap confidences. If I tell you about Jordan, you have to tell me something in return. About Kim, maybe." She knew she was taking a chance on upsetting him by mentioning Kim, but he should talk more about her.

"A bargain, is it?"

"Or nada."

"If I can choose my time, I agree."

He hadn't let her choose her time but she nodded, figuring she'd already won a concession. "Keep in mind you're the only one I've ever told this to," she cautioned.

Steve raised his eyebrows. "I thought women confessed everything to their best woman friend."

"Stereotype!" she accused. "Besides, some things you just don't care to admit. Like how stupid you were to be taken in by a pretty face."

"Pretty?"

"Well, he was. Charmingly persuasive, too. He worked hard to make everyone like him. Most did. Till they got to know him better. Then his incredible shallowness and continual manipulating began to show through. I didn't see any of his faults in the beginning."

"Any virtues?"

She glanced at him, suspecting he might be laughing at her, but his expression verged on grim.

"He was—is—a passable doctor," she admitted.

"So he's still around and about, being charming, I take it."

She nodded. "Why is it impossible to warn some misguided soul about what she's letting herself in for without her believing you're lying because you're jealous?"

"You got warned ahead of time?"

"Obliquely. Naturally I paid no attention."

"You were in love with this jerk?"

Was she imagining the edge to his voice?

"Not fatally, no," she said. "But the realization I wasn't the one and only light of his life hit hard when I read about his engagement to a gal from old Maryland money. I'm ashamed to admit I moped around for weeks until I finally understood how much better off I was without him. It was a painful lesson to learn, not to trust anything a man says. I don't intend to ever make that mistake again."

"What happens when you run across an honest man?"

"Are there any?"

He laid his hand over his heart. "You wound me."

"I'm sure." Since Steve had loosened up, he was fun to be with, something she'd never have suspected when she first knew him. But then she couldn't have imagined their moonlit night at the beginning. Not in a million years.

How easy it had been to tell him about Jordan the Jerk. Maybe because memories of Jordan were fading more rapidly than she'd ever believed possible.

"You shouldn't blame yourself," he said. "Mistaking another person's motives is all too easy."

"It's hard to forgive myself for being too blind to see what he was like and too stubborn to listen to anybody that did know."

"Pretty faces tend to confuse us."

Was he thinking about Kim and himself? Victoria wondered what Kim had really been like. And Steve—had he always had this tendency to withdraw, to conceal?

He hunched forward, focusing on Joker, now curled up sleeping at their feet. "I'm not sure what to do about us," he said slowly. "When we part I don't want you to go off thinking of me as Steve the Deceiver." He offered her a wry smile, then looked away.

"You haven't promised me anything," she said.

"Promises aren't always in words. You must know I want you one hell of a lot."

"That's not a promise."

He took a deep breath and looked directly at her. "More like a bond. Bonds can be harder to break than promises."

Victoria swallowed, her pulse pounding, his words both thrilling and frightening her as she recognized the truth he spoke. "I—I want you, too," she whispered. "It's scary how much."

He reached for her, pulling her up, over and onto his lap, disturbing Joker. The dog sat up and stared at them for a long moment before turning around and settling back down.

"He thinks we're crazy," she murmured into Steve's ear.

"He may be right," Steve told her before his lips covered hers in a hungry kiss.

The day had gone so well, she hadn't thought it could be more perfect. Had she been wrong!

She could stay right here in his lap for the rest of time sharing this kiss with Steve. He tasted of blueberries from the muffins she'd made, and of himself, delicious beyond compare. His lips were warm and compelling as he deepened the kiss, and she felt herself dissolving like sugar in hot coffee.

The trouble with wishing the moment would last forever was, wonderful as the kiss was, she wanted—she needed—more. There might be no moonlight but that didn't matter. What she needed came from Steve, not the moon or the night.

"Damn," he muttered, shifting her slightly, "whoever conceived these miserable Adirondack chairs sure didn't have in mind what I want to do."

Chapter Eight

Joker evidently decided that two people squirming around in one chair needed his attention because Victoria found one of his front feet digging into her thigh. The other was obviously planted somewhere it shouldn't be on Steve.

"Damn!" he cried. "Get down, you mutt!"

When Joker obeyed, Victoria untangled herself from Steve and slid off his lap onto her feet. Steve got up slower, with more effort.

"The time was fine but not the place," he said. "Poor choice. Some chairs are possible but not these wooden monstrosities."

He put an arm around her and led her back inside, with Joker trailing after them. Bevins was complaining loudly about being shut in the shed at what he felt was the wrong time and the dog padded over to sniff at the crack underneath the door.

"Tell me again why you wanted that kitten," Steve said as he let the cat out.

"For the mice, naturally."

"He hasn't caught one yet."

"Caught you, though," she told him.

Steve stopped by the cradle and they both looked down at Heidi, who was awake, making baby sounds.

"If they had goldfish for sale in Hanksville, I might be tempted," he said. "At least fish are quiet and never leave their bowl." He touched Victoria's nose with his forefinger. "We'll have to make it later, in the loft, far away from the vocal and nosy crowd."

Shortly after her evening bottle, Heidi began to fuss and then cry. She wouldn't stop no matter what Victoria did. Finally she decided to try something she'd heard recommended to new mothers. Taking the baby into the bedroom, she kicked off her shoes, then lay on the bed and put Heidi face down on her abdomen with the baby's ear over her heart.

"Don't let me fall asleep," she told Steve, who'd followed her in. "I might roll over."

"Is she all right?" he asked over Heidi's wails. "What're you doing?"

"In the uterus, the baby hears the mother's heart beat continually. I'm hoping my heartbeat will soothe Heidi enough to relax her so she can get rid of what I suspect is gas."

"Colic?"

She nodded.

He left the room and Victoria closed her eyes, rubbing the baby's back gently as she murmured to her. The wails gradually diminished, finally ceasing, but Victoria didn't want to risk moving Heidi just yet. The warm weight on her abdomen was as soothing to her as her heartbeat had been to the baby....

Hearing no sound from the bedroom, Steve ventured in. Heidi looked to be solidly asleep—and so did Victoria. As carefully as he could, he lifted the baby into his arms and eased from the room. Her eyelids fluttered when he laid her in the cradle, so he rocked it gently back and forth, back and forth until he figured she was sleeping soundly again.

He retreated to his chair and picked up the book he'd nearly finished, to pass the time until Victoria roused. Getting involved in the rock 'em, sock 'em, boot 'em, shoot 'em final chapter, he didn't surface until it was all over, with what was left of the good guys as the winners.

Not a sound from the bedroom. He laid the book down and eased over to look at Victoria. She'd turned on her side, away from him, still asleep. He hesitated, then entered the room, lifted the afghan from the footboard rail and spread it over her.

For a long moment he stood there looking down at her, feeling a strange warmth inside that had nothing to do with sex. Shrugging it off, he left the room and, after checking Heidi to make certain she was all right, plucked Bevins off the hearth cushion and shut him in the shed.

That exciting last chapter had reminded him of the exceedingly messy business he and Mikel Starzov had taken care of in Puerto Rico. He liked the guy. New to the agency, Mikel had proved to be one of the best men he'd ever worked with. Seemed to have a sixth sense when it came to ferreting out the rats.

Too keyed up to sleep, Steve decided to go for a walk. "I think Mikel's another loner like me," he told the dog as they headed down the path.

Joker woofed.

"Okay, so I don't qualify as a loner when you're with me," Steve muttered.

Come to that, Victoria and the baby were back at the cabin, along with the cat. He very definitely wasn't alone.

An owl hooted four times off to the left, bringing Joker to a halt. "Stay," Steve ordered, when the dog seemed inclined to investigate.

Joker obeyed, making Steve more positive someone had trained him. He'd have to determine how many basic commands the dog had learned—you never knew when one of them might come in handy.

Not that they weren't safe enough up here on the mountain. He'd never felt so relaxed, except for the times he'd spent in Nevada on the ranch with Karen and her family.

When he finally returned to the cabin, Victoria and Heidi didn't stir when he came in. Apparently he'd be sleeping alone in the loft. He'd planned otherwise but the only way Victoria was going to join him tonight was in his dreams.

Victoria woke with a start, certain someone had called her name. No, not someone—her sister, Renee. In the dark, she was disoriented for the few moments it took her to realize where she was, and it took her still longer to remember why she was fully dressed except for her shoes.

She didn't recall dreaming about Renee and she hoped thinking her sister had called her wasn't some kind of portent. She'd never been in any way, shape or form psychic, so she decided it must have happened because Renee had been on her mind since she'd told Steve about the disappearance.

Victoria got up, turned on the flashlight and left the bedroom to check on Heidi who was sleeping like an angel. The clock told her it was after midnight—Steve must have given up and gone to bed. She returned to her room and undressed, ready to slip into her sleep-T and go back to bed. Instead, she held, struck by a more exciting idea.

Donning her robe, she crept up the steps to the loft with the flashlight lens shielded, allowing just enough light to guide her steps. Once in the loft she clicked it off, letting the moonlight slanting through the windows show her the way to Steve's bed.

She was fascinated by how boyish he looked asleep when there seemed to be only a slight remnant of boyhood within the adult Steve—his sense of fun. And that hadn't surfaced till the other day. Smiling, she set the flashlight on his bedside table, slipped off the robe, let it drop to the floor and started to ease under the covers alongside him.

Instantly he sat bolt upright, startling her so that she let out a squeak of surprise. He grabbed her by the shoulders, hard, hurting. "Steve!" she protested.

"Victoria?" His voice was almost a growl, but his grip eased.

"Who else were you expecting?"

After a short pause he said, "Sorry. Blame it on that thriller I finally finished." He let her go. "I'm not all that accustomed to having beautiful, naked young women crawl into bed with me. As long as you're here, though…" He urged her down along with him until they lay side by side.

"Maybe it was a mistake," she said.

"Never. Did you know I dreamed of you earlier, dreamed you were here in bed with me, just like this?" He turned on his side and pulled her to him.

She found the brush of his chest hair against her bare breasts amazingly erotic. "That was a dream," she murmured. "This isn't. But you didn't know it was me when I arrived in person, so who did you think was in your bed? One of the Adirondack bears?"

"Worse. You don't want to know and I don't want to waste our time explaining." His mouth found hers.

Any desire to go on talking left her as she lost herself in the kiss. Her lips parted to let him come in and ravish her tongue. He was already aroused, she could feel his hardness pressing against her, and she snuggled closer, feeling her own need blossom deep inside her.

"You smell so good," he whispered against her lips.

So did he. His scent was familiar now but that didn't lessen its effect on her. She wanted to lie here forever in his arms, his lips on hers, breathing in his smell, tasting his essence, the silk of his hair under her fingers.

His mouth left hers to kiss his way to her ear. "I didn't plan on us," he murmured. "I didn't stock up on any necessities and we've already taken one chance.''

"No need to worry," she said softly, bemused by his warm breath tickling her ear.

Again they lay in moonlight. She hadn't minded the pine needles the first time, but the bed *was* more comfortable. She ran her hand over the smooth skin of his back, savoring the sensation of the hard muscles beneath the softness. She'd never enjoyed touching a man so much as she did Steve.

Or being touched by him. His every caress tingled through her; he knew just where to explore and how, giving her exquisite thrills and driving her wild with need. Forget tomorrow or next week, or the month after. They were together now, this night, and nothing else mattered.

No woman had ever affected him the way Victoria did. Whatever it was about her—the satiny skin, her perfectly shaped breasts that fit into his hands as though made for them, the sweetness of her mouth— sent him up so high, he could hardly hold back.

The heat of her response when he kissed her and the way her body fit into his made him burn with need. He knew she was more than ready and he was on the cusp himself. He'd wanted to take forever but the night wasn't yet over—there'd be time later for that.

He tore off his pajama pants and flung them aside. "Yes," she whispered as he rose over her. "Yes, now."

Then he was inside her, sheathed in her warmth and she moved with him in perfect rhythm as they showed each other the way to the moon.

When he could think again, he found himself cradling her in his arms, reluctant to let her go. His urgent desire was quieted for the moment but the need to hold her persisted.

"We fit well together," he said softly.

"So perfectly it's scary," she agreed.

Scary? He tested the word. Did it apply to him? He didn't think so. Hadn't they reached an unspoken agreement that this wasn't going to be forever? Maybe she meant the intensity of their coming together. That was something he'd never had before, something he savored.

"Why scary?" he asked.

"I don't like to lose control."

He could go with that; neither did he. "Isn't the loss of control a given in what we're doing?"

"Body control, yes. I meant—well, mental, I guess."

"If you mean when we stop thinking—that's a part of this, too."

"Not exactly the thinking. More a loss of myself."

He understood because he'd experienced a feeling with her, though never before with any other woman, the sensation that they were dissolving into one another. "Strong chemistry," he said.

"I can't argue that point. Look where it's led me." She snuggled closer. "I didn't even like you to begin with."

"So you kept telling me in one way or another." He rubbed his thumb over her nipple, relishing the way it peaked under his caress. "What changed your mind?"

"How can I think when you keep doing that?"

He licked her other nipple, desire creeping up on him again. This time there'd be no rush; this time would last the rest of the night.

Neither of them was prepared for Heidi's predawn hunger call. Victoria reached blindly for the flashlight she'd left on the bedside stand and found herself holding an entirely different object.

"Good grief, it's a gun!" she cried, putting it down as fast as she could and fumbling for the flashlight. She switched it on, glanced at the wicked-looking automatic lying there and turned a questioning gaze on Steve.

"How was I to know you weren't a bear?" he said lightly and, to her ears, evasively. "We'd better get down there and feed the kid before she wears her lungs out."

Though it was heartwarming to have him join her in caring for the baby, the presence of the gun left a sliver of uneasiness festering in her mind. Why did he feel it necessary to keep a pistol on hand when he slept? Was it because of the cabin's isolation? But if that was the reason, why not simply say so?

The pistol on his nightstand nagged at her all the while she changed Heidi, till she finally realized why it had taken on such importance.

She turned to Steve who was warming the bottle and blurted, "The gun was gone, too."

He blinked. "That flew past me. Care to try again?"

"Our father's gun. He always kept it beside his bed. It disappeared the same night Renee did."

"What kind of a gun?" Steve asked.

"A big black revolver with an elk engraved on the brown handle. He said it was a .45 Colt. When he got to drinking, sometimes he'd aim it at us, pretending he was going to shoot. Once the thing actually did go off and the bullet embedded itself in the wall between Renee and me. I'm still terrified of guns."

"Some father you had."

"After my mother and I left, I prayed I'd never see him again."

She picked up the baby from the changing table and walked toward the rocker, disturbed by the tremors cycling through her. So long ago and it still affected her.

"You're trembling," he said. "Take it easy—lie on the couch. I'll feed Heidi."

Victoria handed the baby to him and took his advice. Bevins, who'd been let out of the shed when they first came downstairs, climbed onto her and licked her chin. He settled onto her stomach, purring, when she began petting him. For some reason, the cat's presence comforted her.

"Nothing like a purr," she said shakily.

"I'll try it sometime," Steve said from the rocker. "Do I get to lick your chin, too? Can't promise to stop there, though."

She smiled, the bad vibes fading.

After a time he said, "If it will ease your mind, the gun on the bedside stand bit is a habit of mine. I carry one in my line of work and got into a routine of leaving it there when I went to bed."

Victoria stared at him. "Are you some kind of a cop?"

"You might say so."

"You don't talk much about your work."

"No."

Just a flat *no* without any explanation. But, she decided, it was possible he couldn't discuss what he did. His explanation for keeping the gun close at hand eased her mind. Alice, her psychologist neighbor across the hall in the apartment complex, believed all cops were a tad paranoid. Maybe they had reason to be.

"You'll have to stop leaving your gun out when Heidi gets old enough to be curious about things," she warned.

"I hadn't got that far in my thinking. I do agree kids and guns don't mix."

By the time he finished feeding and burping the baby, Victoria was sitting up, feeling back to normal. As he settled Heidi into the cradle, Victoria carried the kitten back to the shed.

Returning, she stopped beside Steve and said, "I need to be in my own bed for what's left of the night."

He nodded, hugged her and headed for the loft.

Victoria climbed into bed, expecting to lie awake until dawn, but fell asleep within minutes.

Up in the loft, Steve lay awake, upset about Victoria. No wonder seeing the gun had spooked her. If he'd known, he'd have stashed it in the drawer. His mind fixed on the coincidence of her sister and their father's gun vanishing on the same night. Had Victoria's drunken father accidentally shot Renee? Buried her along with the gun?

Steve shook his head, rejecting the scenario. Unless you were way out in the boondocks, someone always heard a gunshot and would have reported it once the police started investigating the girl's disappearance.

Still, it was strange....

He closed his eyes, breathing in the faint traces of Victoria's scent that clung to the bedclothes. She always smelled like flowers. Which reminded him of what she'd said about Willa and the moon blossoms. The moon had set hours ago but it had shone in his windows earlier, silvering Victoria's beautiful body....

Enough of that, he warned himself. Fix your mind on something else or you'll never get to sleep. Think about Nevada, and Karen's extended family. Her husband's twin, Talal, and his wife, Linnea, might be gone from the ranch by now, living in their new house. Linnea had delivered twins several months ago. A wonder Talal didn't insist on his kids being born in Kholi. Probably not safe for him over there yet. Kholi's a strange country.

Kholi. Steve's eyes popped open. *Cold, Kholi.* Very similar. Is *Kholi* the word Kim had said to Victoria? What would link Oni Farraday and Malengo to that Arab country? He'd get the agency on it when he called them from Hanksville later today. He'd give Talal a call, as well.

In the morning sky, the sun flirted with flocks of fleecy white clouds. "Thunderheads by this afternoon," Steve predicted as they left the cabin behind.

"So we may get rained on?" Victoria asked, worrying about the baby in her kangaroo pouch.

"We ought to be back before then. There's not

much reason to hang out in Hanksville, as you'll see.''

Joker, bounding ahead of them on the trail, stopped and looked back to make sure they were still with him. Steve carried a leash in his backpack but had told her that he hoped to control the dog by commands rather than by restraint. She had to agree the dog did obey well—except for escaping when he was tied up.

Victoria decided not to worry about possible rain. The day was pleasantly warm and, though she hadn't minded the cabin's isolation, hiking down the trail felt like a real adventure.

"Is this the only way to get to Hanksville?" she asked.

"Essentially yes, though another trail from Willa's cabin joins this one farther along. If you want to take the van, you have to drive down to Aylestown and go around the mountain to get there."

Which set her off singing "She'll Be Coming Round The Mountain."

"Haven't heard that one in years," he said and, to her surprise, joined in.

Victoria had never felt more lighthearted. Her stressful job was far away, she was in the mountains she loved, with Steve and Heidi and, for the moment, at least, she hadn't a care in the world.

How she loved the scent of the evergreens and the sound of the breeze in their branches. As they descended, from the trees squirrels challenged their right to pass. Peering up to try to spot them, Victoria saw a hawk soaring high above.

Up ahead, Joker started to chase some small animal—a chipmunk?—into the underbrush, but returned on Steve's command to heel. Why, she wondered, had such a well-trained dog become a stray?

She enjoyed every moment of the trek down the mountain but when they reached Hanksville, she saw what Steve meant. Rather than the picturesque village she had in mind, it looked to be a tired, run-down place with the few buildings along the main street badly in need of paint.

"I need to make a couple phone calls," Steve said, stopping at a pay phone by the lone gas station. "The general store's over there." He pointed across the street. "I'll meet you inside."

Seeing the U.S. flag flying from a pole in front of the store, Victoria decided it might also be the post office. She was right. Opening her fanny pack, she removed the sheet of paper she'd scribbled her note to Alice on, bought a stamped envelope at the post office counter and addressed it. Wrapping the note around her key to the mailbox, she slipped it inside, sealed the envelope and pushed it through the mail slot.

Then she wandered through the store, finding a pair of pajamas she thought would fit Steve—maybe he'd get rid of those ratty bottoms then. She picked up various small items, including a brightly colored rattle for Heidi. After paying for everything, she shook the rattle in front of the baby, pleased to note that Heidi was able to focus on the toy. So far the baby showed every evidence of normal development.

"Cute little tyke," the gray-haired woman clerk said. "Got hair as red as yours, I see. Gonna be a handful when she starts walking, I bet."

"She's a handful now," Steve said from behind Victoria.

"Looks just like your wife," the clerk told him.

For some reason Victoria flushed, making him grin at her. As they walked away from the counter, Steve said, "I take it you don't consider that a compliment."

Finding her emotions in turmoil, she didn't reply. What was there to say anyway?

"Are you through in here?" he asked.

She nodded.

"The prettiest spot in Hanksville is up the road a bit," he said. "It's a little park by the river. Unless both picnic tables have fallen into ruin by now, we can eat our sandwiches there."

"And change Heidi," she added.

He rolled his eyes. "Always that. I never realized babies made a career out of elimination."

That made her smile. It seemed he was always making her smile lately.

He bought two cans of soda before they left the store and headed for the park. One, she noticed, was her favorite drink. She hadn't realized he'd paid any attention to what it was.

"Did you get your calls made okay?" she asked.

"Yeah. My sister's brother-in-law, Talal, claims he's being run ragged by their unexpected twins, now around nine months old."

Victoria was willing to take even money that wasn't why he'd called his sister's brother-in-law, but she also knew it was all she was likely to hear about. "Do twins run in the family?" she asked.

"More or less. Talal and my sister Karen's husband

are identical twins. Talal's aren't identical, though. He and Linnea had a boy and a girl. Shas and Ellen.''

"Shas is an unusual name."

"Talal's from Kholi—it was his father's name. Zed's father, too, actually, though Zed was brought up in this country. Rather complicated. Sometime I'll tell you the whole strange story.''

He'd already told her more about himself and his family than she'd ever expected to hear from the Steve she'd met in the beginning. Not that he didn't keep things back. Like the gun.

The little park was empty except for them. Steve used a plastic bag to scrape an accumulation of brown pine needles and other debris from the table that looked to be in the best shape.

Joker, who'd behaved impeccably in the village, not even trying to escape when Steve snapped his leash on and tied him outside the store, waded into the shallows of the river and lapped up water while Victoria changed the baby on the table.

"I really do feel like I'm on vacation," she told Steve. "And one I badly needed."

"You only vaguely resemble that tired, downtrodden nurse I met in the hospital."

She made a face at him. "I might have been tired, but no one trods me down."

He chuckled. "No argument."

They took turns feeding Heidi while they ate themselves. Joker accepted the leftovers with relish.

"Ready for the hike back up the mountain?" he asked.

She nodded.

"None of this 'anything you can do I can do better'

flak,'' he warned. ''If you get winded, say so. We can rest, I can take the baby—whatever.''

''Hey, I may be competitive, but I'm not crazy enough to half kill myself to prove some dubious point. Besides, I already know which is the superior sex.''

Steve grinned at her. Victoria, it occurred to him, had him smiling more in one day then he usually did in a week. Damn it, he was actually happy.

Even what he'd gleaned from talking with the agency couldn't cloud his mood. Mikel Starzov had gotten on the phone and revealed more than the guarded info Steve usually got from the boss.

They suspected a terrorist link between a group in Kholi and some still undiscovered contacts in this country, so what Steve had told Mikel about Kim's message concerning Oni Farraday was gratefully received. Seems she'd been importing Arabian colts from Kholi. They'd look very carefully at the next shipment.

Talal had also been concerned about the situation and said he'd contact his great-uncle, Kholi's king, about Steve's information.

While talking to Mikel, though Steve hadn't meant to bring it up so soon, he'd mentioned the disappearance of Victoria's sister when she was thirteen, describing her and the .45 that had vanished with her. Maybe nothing would come of it, but Mikel was a person who tended to go on picking at a puzzle until he worked out the solution.

''Tell me where the hell you are,'' Mikel had kept insisting. ''If anything happens with Malengo, we don't have a clue to your whereabouts.''

"Nothing will happen. We're safe here."

"Come on, man. Hang it up." Mikel was nothing if not blunt. "You know damn well no one is ever safe."

Unfortunately that had proven true more times than Steve wanted to remember, so he'd finally given Mikel a general idea of the cabin's location.

Talking with Mikel had unsettled him, making him worry about just how safe they were in the cabin. On the other hand, he'd been very very careful and there was really no way Malengo could trace him even to this general area, much less pinpoint the cabin.

As if reading his thoughts, Victoria said, "I feel so safe up here in the mountains. It's a whole different world."

"You *are* safe." He spoke so vehemently, she stared at him in surprise.

"We're all safe," he added more calmly. "Perfectly safe."

But he was no longer as sure about that as he had been.

Chapter Nine

When they got back to the cabin, Willa was sitting in one of the Adirondack chairs in front. Joker bounded up to her and laid his head on her knee to be stroked. Evidently with him it was once a friend, always a friend, Victoria thought.

"Brought you some fresh eggs," Willa said. "Fellow who raises chickens paid me for one of my salves in eggs. Can't use so dang many."

"Thanks," Victoria told her. "We're all out." Victoria was pretty much all worn out after that climb, but added, "Please come in and have something to drink."

"Tea'd suit me," Willa acknowledged, eyeing Steve.

He smiled at her. "A neighbor who arrives bearing fresh eggs is always welcome. I'll even fix the tea."

Willa's expression remained guarded as she said, "Right kind of you. Never did bring you any eggs before in the three years you been coming up here. Wasn't sure you'd want them."

Victoria smiled to herself. Obviously Willa wasn't yet sure she could trust the new, mellower Steve. How thoughtful of him to offer to fix the tea so she could take care of changing Heidi.

When Steve opened the cabin's front door, Bevins scooted out past him and dived into the underbrush. "Guess Joker's not the only escape artist in the family," he said. Then he shook his head slightly, looking momentarily confused.

Because he'd said "family?" Victoria had felt a frisson race along her spine at the word. She'd never expected to hear him use it referring to them, except as a joke. This had slipped out involuntarily, she was sure.

"Joker won't let Bevins get far," Victoria said. The dog was already watching as the kitten eyed him from under a bush.

Inside, Victoria took care of the baby's needs and was cuddling her when Willa said, "Think she'd mind if I held her?"

"Let's try it and see," Victoria told her.

"Best wash my hands first. Been handling them eggs." When she finished, Willa sat in the rocker and Victoria deposited Heidi in her arms.

It was clear from the way she positioned Heidi that this wasn't the first infant Willa had held. The baby seemed perfectly content with where she was.

"Raised up a couple of my brother's young 'uns," Willa said. "Turned out pretty good, they did."

Steve, occupied in the kitchen, said, "One of them wouldn't be Senator Hoover Hawkins, would he?"

Willa grinned. "Smart as a whip, that boy, and fair-to-middling honest, too, once he found he couldn't con me. Course that don't mean he won't try it with the voters."

Steve chuckled. "I'd hate to try to con you, Willa."

"Oh, I reckon you're honest enough," she said. "Just hard to get at."

He raised his eyebrows.

Instead of explaining her remark, Willa focused on Victoria, who was setting the table.

"Victoria, now, she don't hide nothing. Good way to get hurt if you don't take care."

Steve understood from the severe look Willa cast his way that the words were aimed at him. He stared back at her. Didn't the old woman understand he was the last person she needed to warn? He'd never hurt Victoria.

"Tea's ready," he announced.

"Mr. Sandman's come for Miss Heidi," Willa said. "I'll just pop her in the cradle."

Along with the tea, Steve set out a plate with squares of rice cereal bonded together with marshmallows and butter. When Victoria had made it yesterday, after complaining that with no eggs she couldn't concoct any other kind of dessert, the first bite had taken him back to his childhood. He figured his stepmother had first won his trust with the sweet rice cereal squares.

"Favorite of mine," he said now as he took one.

"Coddling him, are you?" Willa asked Victoria.

To Steve's delight, Victoria blushed. He knew it had nothing to do with food but with the other pleasures they'd shared. Ones he meant to share with her again. Soon.

Willa was right about one thing, though—Victoria was an open book. Which was one of the things he liked about her. If Kim had been more like Victoria...

He quashed that thought firmly. Kim had been what she was and now she was gone. He might not be grief-stricken, but he was sorry she was dead.

"Since you did such a good job with Hoover," he said to Willa, "maybe you should be Heidi's honorary grandmother." As he spoke, he realized he'd made a decision he hadn't been aware of until this moment. He was not going to give up Kim's baby. Never to Malengo, but not to anyone else, either. Kim had given Heidi to him and he meant to keep her. Permanently.

Later, as Willa left, Joker brushed past her, coming in through the door, once again holding the kitten in his mouth by the scruff. He deposited Bevins on the hearth cushion and trotted back out again, with the air of one who's done his duty.

"The dog's escorting Willa home," Steve said as he closed the door. "He has his own priorities about what needs doing."

"Just like the rest of us," Victoria said. "My agenda, at this moment, includes taking a nap and nothing else."

It took some effort for Steve not to say, "Great, we'll nap together." But he knew how fatiguing the hike down and back up the mountain could be, especially for someone who hadn't done it before. If they lay down together, there'd be damn little napping done, and she needed to rest.

He nodded. "Go ahead. I'll hold down the fort."

"Protecting the fort does seem to be your agenda," she said, before turning away and entering the bedroom.

Referring to his handgun, no doubt. But then she had no idea what he did or that, even when he wasn't on a case, how the gun sometimes saved his butt. Since he'd picked up another thriller in the general store, he settled down to read it, almost immediately attracting Bevins onto his lap.

"I take it you believe humans exist solely for your benefit," he muttered, fondling the kitten behind its ears. Bevins purred.

A dog, yes—he'd always liked dogs—but he'd never expected to grow fond of a cat. Or a newborn baby—one that wasn't even his. Or the baby's red-haired caretaker. Parting from Victoria wasn't going to be as painless as he'd originally believed.

Again Victoria woke thinking someone had called her name. Since it wasn't dark, she immediately realized where she was, swung her feet off the bed and stood up. In the main room, Heidi was awake but not crying, waving her fists and burbling. Steve sat in a chair reading, with Bevins on his knee and they both looked up at her.

"Did you call me?" she asked.

He shook his head.

Something scratched at the front door. "Joker's home," she said, and let the dog in. He trotted over, peered in at the baby, then curled up on the floor beside the cradle.

"If you didn't call me, I must have been dreaming again," Victoria said. She reached inwardly for the dream but it was gone, the only shard remaining a faint recollection it had been a hospital dream. About Kim.

Only a dream. Alice, the psychologist, would probably tell her the reason she kept feeling she'd been called was unfinished business nagging at her through her dreams. The idea made her uneasy and she set it aside.

Almost immediately she dredged up a comment Willa had made today, and that triggered a memory of something else she'd mentioned at their first meeting. Willa had said Steve had been coming to the cabin for three years and yet she hadn't known he was married till Victoria told her at that first meeting.

"You must never have brought Kim to the cabin," she said.

He frowned. "Didn't I say you were the first person I ever hauled up here with me?"

"Yes, but I didn't know then how long you'd been coming to the cabin."

Silence. Had he retreated into noncommunication again? Willa's comment about hard to get at was right on.

"Kim and I had been growing apart for a long time," he said finally.

Which made Victoria wonder if Kim's getting pregnant had been a failed last-ditch attempt to salvage the marriage. Unfortunately, a baby couldn't unite a couple who had no other ties.

"You don't talk about Kim much," she said.

"No."

Back to monosyllables.

"It might be better if you—" she began before he cut her off.

"I damn well don't care to." The book he'd set on his knee tumbled to the floor. Disturbed, Bevins jumped down and went to investigate his food dish. Joker's head came up, his attention on Steve.

Steve rose and, without another word, headed for the back door, trailed by Joker. They both went out. Heidi began to whimper.

"I don't blame you," Victoria told the baby as she lifted her from the cradle. "Your father in a snit isn't the most wonderful company in the world."

As she was changing diapers, Victoria noticed the day had suddenly gotten much darker. A far-off rumble of thunder told her the reason. Mark up a point for know-it-all Steve, she thought grumpily.

What had she done that was so wrong? Merely mentioned Kim. Settling into the rocker to feed Heidi, Victoria saw Bevins dash across the room and dive under the armoire. Had the cat been chasing something? If it was a mouse and Bevins actually caught it, she hoped the kitten would take it up to the loft and drop it in Steve's bed. Serve him right to bed down with a mouse.

She certainly didn't intend to be in that bed tonight! A flash of lightning lit the cabin's interior with a greenish glow. Thunder crackled ominously close. As rain began to plash against the windows, the back door burst open to admit Steve and Joker.

Victoria wasn't afraid of thunderstorms. Not exactly, anyway. Still, she was glad she wasn't alone up here in this mountain cabin experiencing this one.

Joker came over to sniff at Heidi's toes. Apparently satisfied Victoria wasn't harming her, he trotted over to the armoire and lay down with his nose close to the small space underneath where the kitten still was. At least Victoria hadn't seen him come out.

"Bevins is catching a mouse," she informed Steve, her words intended to show him that she, at least, was above using silence as a weapon.

"Fat chance. They're as big as he is. If he's under that hulking piece of furniture it's because he's intimidated by thunder."

"He is not!"

Steve shrugged and went into the kitchen. "Feel like saying to hell with cholesterol and having scrambled eggs and bacon for supper?" he asked. "I'll be the chef."

She was tempted to tell him that he could lay plaque along the insides of his arteries if he wanted to but she didn't intend to do anything of the sort. Unfortunately, her mouth was already watering at the mere idea. She hadn't eaten bacon and eggs since forever.

Besides, he was offering his own version of an apology. What was the point in denying herself what would be a real treat?

"Just this once," she said.

"You won't be sorry." She saw by the lightning flash he was grinning at her.

How was it possible his grin could send a trickle of desire along her nerve endings? She lay Heidi up against her shoulder, doing her best to concentrate on the baby and ignore him.

Heidi's loud burp brought an admiring "Atta girl" from Steve.

Without warning the storm's intensity increased, wind howling, rain pounding against the cabin, continuous lightning, shattering rolls of thunder. Victoria sprang up from the rocker and, holding tightly to the baby, ran into the kitchen. To Steve.

He put his arms around both her and Heidi, holding them, keeping them safe. Intellectually, Victoria knew very well his arms couldn't actually keep away possible danger from the storm, but emotionally she felt very much protected.

As the storm's fury abated, she eased away from him, embarrassed at what she saw as her lack of courage. "I've never been afraid of a storm before," she said.

"You probably never experienced one in the mountains. They can be awesome."

Somewhat comforted by his assurance that this one was a granddaddy of storms, she returned to the rocker with Heidi who hadn't so much as whimpered the entire time. As she sat down, something small ran across the floor in front of her with Bevins in hot pursuit, Joker bringing up the rear.

If that was a mouse, she was right—but so was Steve. It was almost as big as the kitten.

"Have to admit that cat's heart's in the right place," Steve said as they both watched the race until all three animals plunged though the open door of the shed.

Not long afterward, Bevins and Joker reappeared.

The kitten looked unbearably smug but the dog was the one licking his chops.

"Did you get him, old buddy?" Steve asked Joker.

"We'll never know for sure," Victoria pointed out. "Maybe the mouse got away. For a while there I was hoping Bevins would deposit him in your bed."

"In your place, I take it."

"Something like that," she admitted. "Why are you so prickly?"

"For the same reason you can be a nag."

She bit her lip, thought it over and said, "Okay, so neither of us is perfect. Tell you what—I'll try not to nag if you'll make an effort not to go back into your precabin mode."

"No mice in my bed?"

"I can't speak for Bevins," she said.

"Then I have nothing to worry about. He'll need to double his size before the mice have anything to fear from him."

Joker sat in front of the rocker, head cocked, his attention fixed on Heidi, who offered him another smile.

"Joker—two, Steve and Victoria—zip," Steve said. "Guess we'll have to turn into dogs before we rate a smile from her." He began hauling pans from the cupboard.

The late afternoon brightened as the storm passed by, leaving only a light rain in its wake. As Victoria rocked the baby, a contentment she'd never before experienced settled over her. *Family.* That's what they were, at least for now, and she knew Steve felt it, too.

"Looks like we may get some moonlight later," he said as he beat eggs into froth.

On the surface his words were innocuous enough but Victoria knew very well what he meant. Since they'd made love under the full moon, the moon belonged to them now and moonlight meant lovemaking. Anticipatory warmth settled low inside her and she smiled.

Her smile faded when she remembered the moon was on the wane. There wouldn't be too many more nights before moon dark, just as their nights at the cabin were numbered, and soon the time would come for them to leave and return to reality.

She'd lose Steve and Heidi both. Tears stung her eyes and she blinked them impatiently away. This was something she'd known from the beginning, so why was she obsessing over it?

You're not in love with the man, and the baby is not yours, she told herself firmly. Take what you can and enjoy it, but remember it's only temporary. On loan, so to speak.

Steve's voice jolted her from her musing. "That dog responds to an amazing number of commands," he said. "I'm trying to figure out a way to see if he understands ones for attack like 'Sic 'em' or 'Go get 'em.'"

Joker, who'd lain down beside the rocker, lifted his head and stared at him.

"Look at that!" Steve said. "I think he recognized the words."

Victoria frowned. "Do you need an attack dog for some reason?"

Steve shrugged. "You never know."

"Up here?"

"Joker and I are working out what commands he knows, that's all."

Victoria got the distinct impression he was being evasive. "Is there something I ought to know about?" she asked. "Something you haven't told me?"

"You know all you need to."

Period, she supplied silently. She opened her mouth to protest, then closed it again, determined not to be labeled a nag. She was overreacting. He surely wouldn't have brought Heidi up here if there was any danger.

Seeing that Heidi was asleep, Victoria eased her into the cradle and crossed to the kitchen to set the table.

Later that evening, after the baby had been settled for the night, Steve tied Joker outside the cabin. When he came back in, he captured Bevins, saying, "It's the shed for you, mouser."

Returning from closing Bevins in, he said to Victoria, "The only question remaining is where to put you for the night?"

"Maybe I haven't decided," she said lightly.

"In that case, permit me to make the decision for you." He lifted her into his arms and carried her to the spiral staircase.

"You're not going to try to carry me up that!" she exclaimed, aghast.

"Think of it this way. If we fall, we fall together." He kept on going.

"Men. Should have known better than to make it a challenge," she muttered into his chest.

"Here I am doing my best to be romantic and you're grumbling."

"You didn't blow out the lamps down there," she said.

"Remind me never to get involved with a practical woman again," he teased. "You're supposed to be swooning with admiration at my caveman tactics instead of worrying about kerosene lamps. Don't tell me you expected to be carried up this damn staircase in total darkness."

Victoria giggled.

"Now she's laughing at me," he complained. "There's no pleasing some women. Especially this one who's half strangling me with her death grip."

In the loft, he dropped her unceremoniously onto his bed. "You left your robe up here last night. I hung it on one of the bedposts, in case you care to slip into something more comfortable while I extinguish those blasted lamps."

Steve stripped off his own clothes as soon as he returned to the loft. In the darkness, he found the bed by touch and slid under the covers. "Whoa," he said, "someone's left a naked lady in my bed. Any instructions come with you, ma'am?"

He knew he verged on being silly, a result of being high on the anticipation of coming events, but he didn't care. Victoria would understand; she always did.

"This naked lady is designed for experimentation by the proper naked male," she murmured. "If you are he, what is the password, sir?"

"Moonlight," he told her.

"Oh my, then you must be the one I've been waiting for."

"Give you my word, that's me."

"Do what you will," she whispered. "I'm yours."

The game they were playing had begun to arouse him and her whispered words took him all the way. She *was* his. All night—the devil take tomorrow.

He began with her lips—sweet, seductive and incredibly responsive under his. Slowly and tenderly he kissed his way along her throat and lower, until he reached the soft mounds of her breasts. He caressed one, then the other with his lips and tongue until she began to moan, then continued his journey on down.

When he reached his goal, he gently urged her legs apart until they opened, offering him access. Hot and throbbing though he was by now, he refused to hurry. Placing his hands under the enticing curves of her buttocks and raising her, he took his time as he pleasured her.

Her incoherent words mixed with gasps not only told him she was on the cusp, but fired his own need to an almost unbearable pitch. When she cried out, he lost the ability to prolong his wait and rose above her, plunging into her moist and welcoming warmth, feeling her draw him deeper and deeper.

She called his name, her voice rising to a near scream. He wanted to tell her, needed to tell her…but it was too late for words. He couldn't speak, he could only cry out as she had done, joining her in the final journey.

Only when he returned to awareness and eased from her onto his side, pulling her into his arms, did he realize they were bathed in moonlight.

After a time, she murmured, "When does the naked lady get her turn?"

He grinned, hugging her closer. There was no other woman like Victoria. "This particular moonlight lady can have her turn anytime she chooses, no-holds-barred," he told her.

What she did to him was positively indecent, and he enjoyed every second of it, from the nibbling at his nipples to the way she caressed more arousing spots than he knew he possessed.

She had him exactly where she wanted him by the time she straddled his body and eased herself down onto his all-time-high arousal. He was more than ready for a wild ride to the moon. Instead, she teased him by almost withdrawing and then sliding down again with agonizing slowness.

When he tried to speed things up, she leaned down to his ear and told him, in a husky whisper that did nothing to improve matters, that it was her turn, not his.

He was ready to explode by the time she lost her own control and let him take them both on the tumultuous ride he could tell she needed as desperately as he did.

Lying there spent, with her in his arms, he knew he'd never forget this night. When he regained enough energy to form words, he asked, "Who gets the next turn?"

"Offhand, I'd say Mr. Sandman," she said drowsily.

"Okay, but he better not forget just who this naked lady belongs to."

"Don't belong to anyone but myself." Her words were so slurred, he knew she was sliding into sleep.

It was true. He'd have said the same if she'd claimed him as hers. Yet, for the first time in his life he understood the meaning of being bonded to someone else, because they were, he and Victoria.

Chapter Ten

Steve woke to darkness, the moonlight gone. Victoria, though, was still there, cuddled up against him, one arm flung across his chest. Unlike Kim, who'd always turned away from him once they'd had sex.

He'd realized soon after she left him, that what he and Kim shared had been lust, not love. They'd never really liked one another except superficially. No wonder the marriage split apart. As his grandmother had commented, "Marry in haste, repent at leisure."

When she left him for Malengo his pride was more wounded than his heart. He didn't understand why any woman would choose a scumbag like that. No matter how handsome the surface, he felt Malengo's essential slimy nature showed through the fake charm and designer clothes.

But then, he wasn't a woman. He knew the guy

had used fast-lane romance to net Kim because the agency had traced several of their clandestine meetings prior to the split. Always in some expensive resort designed for "lovers." Steve, himself, had never been the romantic type—not until lately, with Victoria. Somehow she inspired it.

"Victoria," he said softly, enjoying the sound of her name.

He felt her start and then tense. "It's okay," he murmured, "you're with me."

"I thought I heard someone call my name."

"This time you were right. I did."

"No," she said, "in my dream it was a woman. Kim, I think."

"Why would you dream of her?"

"Alice says most dreams are unfinished business the dreamer's unconscious is still trying to settle."

"Who's Alice?"

"My apartment neighbor across the hall—a psychologist."

"What's she have to do with Kim?"

Victoria sighed. "Nothing. I guess maybe Kim's on my mind because I'm with you."

Steve made a decision. There were many things he couldn't tell anyone, even Victoria, but he thought she deserved the truth about his marriage to Kim.

"Our divorce was final three years ago," he said bluntly. "I hadn't seen Kim since then, until I was called to the hospital a couple of weeks ago."

After a moment of silence, Victoria said, "If that's true, what about the baby? You can't possibly be her father."

"I'm convinced Kim named me as Heidi's father

because she wanted me to protect the baby from Heidi's real father. I don't have a clue why she intended to do that. When you handed me Heidi at the hospital I was dumbfounded, at a complete loss. At the time none of it made sense to me.''

"I knew you were in shock." Victoria drew away from him until there was a space between them. "I was wrong as to why, though.''

"I couldn't tell anyone, you included, I wasn't the real father, until I worked out why Kim would have lied to the hospital about it. At that time, I thought you'd only be with us—with me and the baby—temporarily.''

"I *am* only temporary." As she spoke, he could sense Victoria propping herself up on her pillow.

"You know what I mean. In the beginning I didn't intend to come up here and we both thought I'd be hiring a more permanent baby nurse." He sat up and punched his pillow until he was comfortable leaning back against the headboard.

"You've got it all worked out now?" she asked.

"More or less.''

"Why did Kim do it, then?''

"I can't tell you.''

"So you're back to being Mr. Mystery.''

"Damn it! I don't discuss my job with anyone!''

That should shut her up, he thought with increasing annoyance. Why does she have to poke and pry? Kim had tried to do the same thing—without results.

"I don't understand how all this can be related to whatever it is you do," Victoria said finally.

"You never will," he told her.

"Period," she snapped.

"Yes, if you insist. Until I married Kim I never really understood that Bluebeard fairy tale about all the wives. But I've gradually come to see he wasn't the unreasonable monster I once thought. Women are too damn inquisitive for their own good."

"No wonder Kim left you." Her voice quivered with outrage.

"Go ahead, cast me in the role of Bluebeard. You still won't get any answers I feel are none of your business."

That did it! Victoria flung back the covers, groped for her robe hanging on the bedpost, slid into it and felt her way to the door.

"Wait, take the flashlight."

"No!" she all but shouted. "I might get your damn gun by mistake and I'd hate to be responsible for shooting you."

She found the first step of the staircase and descended carefully, despite her eagerness to get as far away from him as possible. Falling down this spiral monstrosity in the dark wasn't on her agenda.

She had difficulty accepting the fact that Heidi wasn't his daughter. And that, for reasons he wouldn't divulge, he was keeping the baby away from the man who had fathered her. Which made her Steve's accomplice, didn't it? She had been all along, inadvertent or not.

His was a lie by omission, granted, because now that she thought about it, he'd never actually claimed to be the baby's father. But it was a lie all the same. What else had he failed to tell her?

If it were possible to get out of this snarl easily, she'd bolt tonight. But even if she could leave right away, the one to suffer the most would be Heidi. For the baby's sake, Victoria's only choice was to stay on top of this mountain till Steve brought them back to civilization.

As soon as that happened, she'd take it upon herself to make a list of reputable agencies where he could hire a caretaker, present it to him and tell him in no uncertain terms she was leaving. If he didn't call one of the agencies immediately and make other arrangements, she'd damn well do it for him.

Settling herself in her own bed, Victoria tried to make sense of what he'd told her. In the hospital, she'd known Kim was frightened, but who wouldn't be, badly injured and in labor. Had Kim had an additional reason to be afraid? It was impossible to tell.

Henderson had been the name on her driver's license, the same as Steve's, which indicated she hadn't married again. What about the man who'd fathered Heidi? Steve obviously knew who he was and didn't like him. Why? Jealousy was the obvious answer, but—after three years apart from Kim? Could this man somehow be associated with Steve's job?

What *was* his job? Something to do with law enforcement. If Heidi's father was on the wrong side of the law... Victoria shifted uneasily. Is that why they'd come to the cabin? To hide from this man?

It hadn't seemed particularly odd at the time, but she recalled how Steve had switched from the car to the van, how he'd used what had seemed like a circuitous route and now these things took on a new significance. He could have been making certain they hadn't been followed.

Apparently they hadn't been and, if so, they should

be safe in this isolated cabin. He'd bought it after his divorce. Which meant Kim wouldn't have known about the cabin and so couldn't have told anyone. Joker must have been acquired as an added safety precaution.

But why couldn't Steve have explained all this to her? Once they were up here, even if she'd been inclined to tell anyone, how could she? Maybe he thought she'd blab to Willa. No, he wouldn't have gotten to the point of worrying about that because Steve Henderson just plain kept everything to himself on general principles.

Yet, for some reason she couldn't fathom, he'd finally told her about divorcing Kim three years ago.

Unable to sleep, Victoria was relieved when Heidi woke for her early-morning feeding because it gave her something to do. When she finished with the baby and had her settled again, Victoria fell into bed and into sleep's welcome oblivion.

She woke in the late morning and found that Steve, who was not in the cabin, had already taken care of Heidi. The van was gone, as was her list of needed supplies, so she knew he must have driven down to Aylestown to stock up. Neither Bevins nor Joker was inside. After she ate a quick breakfast, she went out to look for the kitten and found him sleeping on a shirt Steve had left in one of the Adirondack chairs. Joker bounded up to her, tail wagging.

The morning, rain-washed fresh and clean, was coolish but pleasant. Feeling restless, Victoria decided to put on the pouch and take Heidi and herself to visit Willa. Before she left, she scrawled a terse note for Steve to let him know where they were.

Shutting the kitten in the cabin, she set off with Joker and Heidi. Before she'd gone a tenth of a mile, the blue jay she'd begun to call the guard bird sent up a clamor, following them till they left the territory he regarded as his. Despite her somber mood, the mountain air and the exercise lifted her spirits.

Willa seemed pleased to see them. "I didn't reckon on Steve bringing me such good company," she said. "Good for him, too," she added, smiling.

"I take it he didn't talk to you much in past years," Victoria said.

"Nothing over what was necessary. Glad to see the change."

Much as she wanted to unburden herself to Willa, Victoria knew she must not. She might know only a small part of Steve's secret but it was his and not hers to talk about.

"We'll set a bit," Willa said. Her two Adirondack chairs in front were identical to the ones at Steve's cabin except for being padded with faded chintz cushions, making them more comfortable.

Victoria lifted the baby from the pouch onto her lap where she could kick to her heart's content. "There's no scale around," she said, "but I can tell she's getting heavier every day."

"Lively young'un. You staying on with her once he leaves here?"

Victoria shook her head. "I have a job to go back to." Her voice must have given her away, because Willa reached over and patted her knee.

"Most men are dang fools. Every so often one of 'em smartens up some. Could be he will."

Victoria tried to find words to deny any interest in

Steve other than as an employer but they stuck in her
throat. Peeved as she was at him, she couldn't shake
the unhappy feeling that the ties between them would
be all but impossible for her to sever.

"Never you mind, gal. If 'tis meant to be, 'twill
be. He needs you—'tis plain for all to see, 'cept
maybe him.''

If Steve did need her, it was only to take care of
Heidi, and he could find another caretaker for that.
Victoria gazed down at the baby, her heart full of
love, wondering how she could bear to give Heidi up.
The baby focused on her and smiled.

Victoria burst into tears. She felt Willa pluck Heidi
off her lap and tried to regain control of herself, but
could not. She wasn't one to cry, having learned as a
child it did no good, but lately she'd turned into a
regular weeping willow.

Willa thrust a folded cloth into her hands and, when
the tears lessened, Victoria used it to wipe her wet
face, discovering it was a red bandanna. When she
could speak, she said, "I'm not crying over him. It's
having to give up the baby I can't bear."

"So you don't care a fig for Steve."

Willa's words seem to hang in the air between
them, demanding a response, but Victoria couldn't
make herself reply because she didn't know what to
say. How did she feel about him?

He was a wonderful lover. She'd grant him that.
No other man would ever match Steve. But that didn't
mean she'd fallen in love with him. Never!

"Guess we got the answer," Willa said, pretending
to be talking to the baby. "You got to remember,
Miss Heidi, that there ain't no maybe when it comes

to loving a man. Either you do or you don't. And when you can't say you don't, then like as not you do.''

Deciding a denial now would be too little, too late, Victoria kept quiet, watching the baby eye Willa solemnly. She was just about to reach to take her back when Heidi offered Willa a smile.

"'Tis a wise child you got here,'' Willa said, returning her to Victoria. ''She agrees with me.''

Victoria scarcely heard the last words because she'd gone on to mentally finish Willa's first words. *It's a wise child who knows its own father.* Fighting an urge to laugh hysterically, she cuddled the baby to her. What would become of this precious child?

By the time she returned to the cabin, Steve was there. ''How was Willa?'' he asked.

''Heidi smiled at her,'' Victoria told him. ''At me, too.''

''And you figure it serves me right if she never smiles at me, is that it?''

Damn the man. He could sabotage a good mad quicker than anyone she'd ever met. Not that she intended to forgive him, but sniping was silly.

''Got everything on the list,'' he said, handing it back to her with all items checked off.

Glancing over it, she saw with dismay she hadn't added baby vitamins as she'd meant to—yesterday she'd used the last of the sample bottle the hospital had sent home with Heidi.

''I forgot to put down vitamins for the baby,'' she confessed. ''She does need them.''

"If it can wait, I'll be needing to make another phone call in a day or two."

"No problem. She can go several days without vitamins. In the old days there weren't any such thing and babies not only survived, they thrived."

He nodded. "Still thinking of shooting me?"

"I wouldn't know how if I did want to," she countered. "I've never held a gun in my hand until the other night when I accidentally grabbed yours."

"Not even that old Colt of your father's?"

"I was terrified of that gun. Renee picked it up once when he was gone and I ran off like a scared rabbit."

Steve filed her comment away. Renee evidently hadn't been afraid to touch the Colt. He followed Victoria to the changing table.

"You didn't happen to have lunch at Willa's, did you?" he asked.

She shook her head. "Tea and sympathy."

He let that lay. "Good. I brought back a surprise for lunch. When you get Heidi settled we'll eat."

He wanted to please her—needed to—which bothered him. When did he change from not caring one way or the other about the nurse he'd hired to look after Kim's baby? For that matter, when and how had he come to think of Heidi as *his* baby? Or what was even more disturbing, Victoria as his?

"I really do feel like Bluebeard," he said.

She shot him a puzzled look. "Why?"

"It has to do with trust."

Victoria picked up the freshly changed baby and retrieved the warmed bottle. As she walked past him toward the rocker, she said, "Trust goes both ways or none. I never did like that fairy tale."

While she fed the baby, he smuggled the box in from the van by putting it in a black plastic bag. In the kitchen he eased it from the bag and placed box and all in the warming oven of the stove.

After a time Victoria lifted her head and sniffed. "Something smells good enough to eat."

He grinned at her, wanting things between them to be as they had been yesterday, before he decided to tell her about the divorce and how long ago it had been. He should have kept his mouth shut.

When she leaned over to put Heidi into the cradle, he took the box from the oven and laid it on the table he'd already set. Placing two cold sodas—one her favorite—beside the glasses, he crossed to the cradle and offered her his arm.

"Milady, luncheon awaits."

She smiled and took his arm, allowing him to lead her to the table where, after seating her, he opened the box with a flourish.

"Pizza!" she cried. "With all the stuff on it I love."

Surprising her with something he knew she liked was his way of telling her he was sorry he'd upset her last night. Did she realize that? He thought she probably did—not much escaped her.

He waited until they'd both eaten their fill before saying, "I want you to understand that if I could tell you any more than I already have, I would. The agency I work for expects us to keep secrets."

Her gaze held his. "What you did tell me was a shock. I had to revise everything I believed to be true about you, Heidi and Kim. I felt you'd lied to me— by omission at least. Kim did want you to have the baby, though. That I know, even if not why."

"I felt I had no choice at the time."

She nodded. "I'm still mulling over your Blue- beard reference. He killed all those poor wives for merely being curious—what a monster! The last wife finally outsmarted him, though."

"Not really, though she did have enough sense to have a backup plan in case she needed help. Her brothers riding to the rescue is what saved her."

"I won't quibble. But why do you feel like Blue- beard?"

"Women's curiosity drove him to his monstrous deeds and I have some empathy for the poor guy. Here I am having to fend off your curiosity like I did Kim's. One of the reasons she left was her inability to accept the fact I can't talk about what I do at work. Not at all. Women can't seem to bridle their curios- ity."

Victoria held up her hand. "Stop right there. I'll admit humans, as a race, are curious but women are no more so than men. And I'm not women, I'm me. So, okay, your work is secret—fine. I don't want to know anything about it. But getting information that isn't secret out of you makes me feel like a dentist trying to yank out an impacted tooth."

He blinked at her. "What information?"

"Any and all. Your instinct seems to be to hide as much as you can so I have to guess at things."

"I've told you things about myself." He sounded defensive, even to himself, but plowed on. "You know about my sister, Karen, and my parents."

"That's 'cause we were trading family info. You hardly ever volunteer any. On the rare occasions that you do drop a crumb, I feel it must have slipped past the barrier accidentally."

The rein on his anger slipped and his voice rose. "I don't know what the hell you expect me to tell you."

Heidi began to whimper.

"You scared her," Victoria accused, getting up and hurrying to the cradle.

"Sure, blame Bluebeard," he muttered, pushing away from the table.

Holding the baby, she turned to face him. "If you think I'm going to stand on a parapet staring down the road looking to see if anyone's riding to the rescue, you couldn't be more wrong. I'm capable of taking care of myself, thank you."

"I never doubted that. Anyway, the cabin doesn't happen to have even one parapet, which I believe is the wall around what you're not going to stand on."

"Whatever," she snapped. "You know what I mean."

Heidi's fussing grew louder.

"You're upsetting her as much as I am," he said.

He watched her take a deep breath and knew she was trying to calm herself, and his annoyance ebbed. How could he stay angry at this woman who amused him as much as she irritated him?

"How about letting me take my turn with my daughter?" He used "my" deliberately.

Wordlessly she held out the baby to him.

Seating himself in the rocker, he put the chair into motion, back and forth, back and forth, and began to speak softly to the fussy baby. "Hey, little girl, I don't mind a real cry if you need something, but this whimpering is out. You've got two people here at your beck and call, a dog to protect you and, when you get a bit older, a cat to amuse you."

Heidi's gaze settled on his face and she stopped fussing.

He went on talking to her. "I'll bet if old Bluebeard had happened to have a cute little daughter like you to hold, he wouldn't have wanted to murder all those nosy ladies. He might even have shaved."

He heard Victoria giggle but didn't take his attention from Heidi.

"So how about a smile for your poor old dad after you made him feel guilty for upsetting you? What kind of a kid are you anyway?—the dog gets a smile, Willa gets one, too, then Victoria. Here's how it goes, in case you need reminding." He grinned at her.

Heidi gave him an endearing, toothless smile.

"Atta girl," he said, cuddling her, trying to hide how affected he was.

He held her, rocking back and forth, until she fell asleep.

After he laid her in the cradle, he looked around. Victoria was not in the cabin, so he collected Bevins and put him down outside. Victoria sat in one of the Adirondack chairs with Joker at her feet.

"I'd like to get some pads for these chairs," she said.

"I'm with you. Maybe the general store in Hanksville will have some—we'll be hiking down there the day after tomorrow. Want to take a short walk now? The Sandman came for Miss Heidi."

"Willa does have a neat way of expressing herself," Victoria said, rising. "I'll miss her."

As they strolled along the trail, to his surprise, Steve found himself realizing he'd miss Willa, too. That's what happened when you let anyone start edging past the barrier. And Victoria was all the way in. What was he going to do about Victoria?

As if reading his mind, she said, "What do you intend to do about permanent care for Heidi when we go back to the city?"

"I haven't decided," he admitted.

He half listened to her mention of caretaker services, his mind fixed on how he might persuade her to stay on. And on. And on...

Chapter Eleven

As Victoria was getting ready for bed that evening, she noticed the package from the general store on her dresser and realized what it was. She'd been waiting for the right moment to present Steve with the new pajamas she'd bought for him in Hanksville and had totally forgotten they were there.

Standing there in her sleep-T, she tried to decide whether to wait until tomorrow or not. There'd been sort of an unspoken agreement that they'd sleep in separate beds tonight, and she didn't want him to think she was changing the parameters.

If she'd remembered earlier, she could have snuck upstairs while he was tying Joker out in back and put the new pajamas on his bed for him to find when he went up to the loft. She'd missed that chance but, since he was still sitting in the main room reading his new thriller, she could pop out, drop the pj's in his lap and zip back into her room. To be polite, he'd probably wear them tonight, which meant just maybe he'd get rid of those grungy old bottoms.

No need to put on her robe for the quick dash she intended to make. Smiling in anticipation of his surprise, she eased out of her room, watching to see if he'd noticed her. Bevins, on his knee, looked at her, but Steve's attention remained on his book. She tiptoed across to the chair and was preparing to drape the pajamas over the thriller when he snaked out a hand, grabbed her and flung her onto him.

The book thudded to the floor and Bevins fled with an indignant yowl as Steve adjusted her until she was sitting in his lap.

"You are *so* sneaky," she complained, tugging at the bottom of her sleep-T. "I'll bet you knew I was there all the time."

"I don't like to be surprised—but this could be an exception."

"The surprise was supposed to be these." She dug the pajamas out from under her and shook the bottoms at him. "Heidi and I bought them for you in Hanksville."

He grinned. "I can't imagine why."

"We felt we had to do something before what seems to be your only pajama bottom completely disintegrates."

"You don't like naked men?"

"I find that a leading question." Sitting in his lap wasn't conducive to clear thinking. Especially with one of his hands caressing her bare thigh.

"Leading where?" His fingers crept under the bottom edge of her nightshirt.

"Sir, are you making indecent advances?" she asked.

"Wouldn't dream of any such thing, milady. An advance, yes. Indecent, never." His fingers crept higher.

She hadn't meant to slip into a fantasy role but couldn't help herself. He not only made her feel desire, he also made her feel desirable. A fatal combination.

"I'll agree to wear the new bottoms if you'll promise to wear the top," he said.

"But it'll be too short."

"Exactly."

She'd walked into that one. Now he was one up. "Don't you want to get back to your book?" she asked.

"What do you think?" His hand reached the juncture of her thighs.

"Given what you're doing, I'm not too sure I can," she confessed, tingling all over with increasing need.

"Good. Because unlike the Adirondack ones, this chair is the right kind."

"Um—for what?"

"It's a case of showing, not telling." He kissed her, hot and hard and hungry.

Victoria gave herself up to pure pleasure. She might not see eye to eye with Steve on everything but they melded perfectly when it came to making love. His caresses turned her insides to lava, hot and steamy.

He slid down farther in the chair. "Think you can

figure out what to do?'' His voice, low and husky with need, thrilled through her.

She managed to get the zipper down on his jeans without permanently disabling him. When his arousal was free of clothes, she stroked him gently until he put an end to it by raising her up until she was poised just right above him.

Taking him inside her, she gasped his name, overcome with wildly escalating sensations.

As she enclosed him, he tried to say how wonderful it felt, but he'd gone too high too fast and his mind wouldn't form words.

Together on this erotic journey, that's the way it should be, would always be....

They clung together afterward until both were in danger of sliding off the chair onto the floor. Reluctantly he let her pull away from him and stand up while he eased back into the chair.

''All I was really trying to do was give you the new pajamas,'' she told him.

''At the moment I'm willing to believe anything you tell me.'' He dug down into the chair and produced the top. ''All yours.''

She took it, leaned down and kissed him lightly. ''Good night, Steve.'' Her voice was a caress.

He watched her go into the bedroom and come out again almost immediately holding Bevins. ''Look who thought he was going to sleep with me,'' she said, heading for the shed, where she shut the kitten in.

''If I don't get to, no other male does,'' he said.

She slanted him a look of mock disapproval and disappeared into her room. Amazing how much he

enjoyed watching her. Victoria was not one to fuss
around; she did everything with an economy of motion he found fascinating. As well as being open, she
was stimulating to be with. Refreshing. And fun. He'd
forgotten women like her existed. Or maybe he'd
never known they did.

He smiled, reflecting on their lovemaking. Though
he'd have liked Victoria to share his bed tonight, he
hadn't expected she would after their disagreement
earlier. What happened was a real bonus. Being un-
planned made it all the more exciting. Not that every
time they made love wasn't an event in itself.

Remembering how she'd fled to him when that
awesome storm was at its peak warmed him. As in-
dependent and capable as she was, she'd needed the
comfort of his arms. He found himself fervently wishing their time at the cabin would never end.

He knew that sooner or later they had to leave, but
he didn't want to think about it.

Getting up, he grabbed the flashlight, snuffed the
lamp and climbed to the loft with his new pajama
bottoms.

When the baby's first piercing wail woke him,
Steve couldn't believe he'd been to sleep at all. The
illuminated dial of his watch told him he was wrong.
He yawned, climbed out of bed and flicked on the
flashlight. Three o'clock in the morning had never
been his favorite time of day. The slight thrumming
on the roof told him it was raining again, though not
too hard.

Downstairs, a tousle-haired, sleepy-looking Victoria was just lifting Heidi from the cradle, so he padded

into the kitchen to warm a bottle. He watched her change the baby, thinking no matter what she wore or didn't wear, no matter what time of the day or night, Victoria was a beautiful woman.

As he sat in the rocker with the warmed bottle, Victoria said, "I've always believed breast-feeding is important if a mother can do it, but I also see the advantages of trading off sometimes."

She handed him the baby and curled up on the couch, yawning. "You're wearing the new bottoms," she said. "Good."

"I was afraid not to."

"Ha! I doubt that. I'll never see the day when Steve Henderson is afraid of me."

He shifted Heidi to a more comfortable position and made sure she was sucking steadily on the nipple, then frowned at Victoria. "You reneged."

She blinked. "Oh, you mean because I'm not wearing the top? I want you to know I'm saving it for a special occasion."

"With me?"

"You'll just have to wait and see." She yawned again.

"Why don't you go back to bed? I can handle Heidi."

"I know that. But I was having a bad dream when she woke me, a dream I was glad to get out of. I don't want to risk slipping back into it."

"That bad?"

She nodded. "Renee was trying to reach me in the dream, but I couldn't find her. I guess the dreams are happening because talking about her to you somehow brought her back to my mind. I'm not a bit psychic."

"Just as well. You have enough talents without adding that one. About Renee—do you have any idea at all where she might have gone if she left on her own?"

"I want to believe she did that. It's too horrible to think about any other alternative."

"Did she ever talk about where she'd like to go if she could?"

Victoria shrugged. "Sure—Paris, Venice, Jamaica, Finland...."

"Finland?"

"She had a crush on one of the male teachers in school who was Finnish."

"Did he ever respond, do you think?"

"Mr. Saari?" Victoria frowned. "I don't think so, but I really don't know 'cause she'd moved up to middle school by then and I was still in elementary. But he was at least thirty and Renee was only thirteen."

"We both know age doesn't count with some men."

Victoria grimaced. "Do you mind if we talk about something else?"

"Sorry. Unsolved mysteries intrigue me."

"Must be why you work for this secret agency."

Now she'd hit on something he didn't care to discuss. He filed away Saari's name and decided to go back to what had set them at odds yesterday.

"Have you come to terms with me not being Heidi's birth father?" he asked.

She crossed her arms over her breasts. "I'm not sure. I hate dealing with lies, even when they're by omission."

"Would you have agreed to come and take care of Heidi if you'd known everything at the beginning?"

"How can I answer that? I'm so attached to her now that I can't say what I might have done back then."

If she hadn't decided to come with him, they wouldn't have had this interlude of intimacy, something he'd never forget.

"You're one sexy woman," he said.

Her blush made him smile.

Victoria put her hands to her hot face. "The curse of being a redhead," she muttered.

"Not all redheaded women are sexy," he said, deliberately misunderstanding her to provoke a reaction.

"You know what I mean!" She glared at him, then shook her head, obviously realizing she'd been had. "You got me again, so now you're two up. Just you wait."

He grinned, pleased to have lured her from the gloomy aftermath of her dream into a lighter mood.

When at last Heidi, clean and dry, fed and burped, finally succumbed to Mr. Sandman, Steve laid her gently in the cradle and covered her. He offered his hand to help Victoria rise from the couch, but she ignored it, getting up on her own. He took the hint. Separate beds for the rest of the night.

He could hardly complain, considering, but he longed to have her beside him. Not only for the lovemaking, but because it was beginning to feel right to know she was there, even when asleep.

When Victoria woke the next morning, she saw the sky was overcast, though the rain had stopped. Before noon, though, a drizzle began, as much mist as rain but wet all the same.

"Looks like an indoor day up here," Steve said. "Might be better down in Aylestown—sometimes the mountain gets bad weather when the valley doesn't. We could take a spin and see. You could pick up those baby vitamins and look for chair pads. Whatever."

"Sounds good to me," she said. "I'll get Heidi ready."

After the baby was strapped into the back seat carrier and they were settled in the front, Steve started the van, cursed and turned off the engine.

"Something the matter?" she asked.

"The add oil light came on. Have to check the level."

He got out and lifted the hood. After a few minutes he returned, scowling. "No oil in the damn thing. The warning light must be faulty or I'd have noticed before now."

Victoria knew enough about cars to realize if you drove one that was out of oil you risked seizing the engine.

"What are we going to do?" she asked.

"Nothing for it but to hike down the hill to Hanksville and pick up a couple quarts," he said.

"In the rain?"

"It's not an emergency. We'll wait until the rain stops."

The discovery the van was out of oil left Steve in such a bleak mood she hesitated to initiate any conversation that wasn't essential. She understood he blamed himself, which she thought was foolish. Sure, he could have kept a can of oil around for emergencies, but it was no big deal that he hadn't.

Finally the silence drove her into speech. She stalked over to where he was gloomily gazing out at the drizzle and demanded, "Why do you have to be such a perfectionist? Things like this happen to everyone."

"Not to me," he said grimly, turning to look at her. "Slipups like this could get a man killed."

Victoria rolled her eyes. "That's carrying it a tad far. So you depended on the add oil light to warn you when the supply ran low, and it malfunctioned. Is that your fault?"

"I could have checked the oil level more often," he muttered.

"You told me we were in no danger here at the cabin. What does it matter that we have to wait until tomorrow to get oil so we can have wheels again? You said yourself there's no emergency."

"None I can foresee, but then emergencies tend to be unforeseeable."

"Okay, no argument there. But no one is perfect. If you were, people wouldn't be able to stand you— me included. Maybe your father expected you to be, but you certainly must know that's an impossible goal by now. Perfection for any human being is unobtainable."

That got a reluctant grin out of him. "Are you telling me you like me exactly the way I am?"

"Well, if I could, I'd make a few changes here and there. Perfection isn't one of them, though."

He didn't say anything for a time, so she went into

the kitchen to see about lunch. He followed her, saying, "I hate being stuck indoors."

"So go out and chop wood. A few drops of rain won't melt you."

"I can see you're fresh out of sympathy."

Joker, who'd been sleeping by the baby's cradle, got up and ambled to the front door, asking to be let out. Steve obliged, then said, "When he comes back in we'll get to smell wet dog. What a treat."

"Whatever is the matter with you?" Victoria demanded, exasperated. "I never expected you to be a moper."

Steve shook his head. "A moper. What a label. Okay, guilty. I'm just not used to failing."

She turned with a wooden spoon in her hand and shook it at him. "I'm not going over that again. It's your father's voice saying you failed, not mine and not the voice of reason. Let it go, can't you?"

About to make a crack about how living across the hall from Alice the psychologist had influenced her, Steve held back his words. *His father's voice?* He went back to the window to think that one over.

Whether she was right or not, he decided, he was behaving more like a ten-year-old than an adult. Get over it, Henderson, he chided himself.

The mention of his father had triggered a errant memory. "Do you play cribbage?" he asked.

"I've heard of the game. That's about it," she told him. "Why?"

"I just remembered that a cribbage board and a deck of old cards came with the cabin. My dad taught me when I was a kid. Haven't played in years, but we could give it a whirl. Beats moping."

She gave him a quick smile. "Most anything does."

After lunch, he got out the board and the little pegs to keep track of the players' scores. Victoria proved to have a knack for the game and they played most of the afternoon with time out for Heidi. The end result was a tied score and an improved mood as far as Steve was concerned. He'd actually had fun.

By nightfall the drizzle had ceased, though clouds still hung low on the mountain. Victoria began to wonder if Steve was going to ask her to spend the night in his bed and, if he did, what she was going to say. She was no longer angry with him but it still hurt that he'd violated her trust. First, by not being completely honest from the beginning, and secondly, by not trusting her enough to tell her the truth much earlier than he finally had.

Last night's lovemaking in the chair had been wild and unexpected—she hadn't had time to make a conscious choice. Thinking about it made her knees weak, but that didn't mean she'd say yes if he invited her into his bed tonight.

He could call her a sexy lady all he wanted to but she certainly didn't intend to made any such offer to him. Or even accept his. Not until she was clearer in her mind about everything that had gone on between them since the beginning.

When time came to go to bed and he hadn't indicated in any way whether he intended to sleep alone or planned to ask her to join him, Victoria refused to accept her disappointment. This way made it easier, after all.

She had to admit to some regrets, though, when she curled up alone in her own bed. No matter how reluctant her mind might be, her body definitely wanted to be in his bed rather than this one.

The following morning turned out to be clear and sunny, but the foliage was so wet they put off the hike to Hanksville until the afternoon to give things a chance to dry off.

Willa came by before noon with a mess of green beans from her garden. Invited inside, she sat down and said, "Dang things all ripen at once and I'm not canning this year. The more I got to thinking on it, the more I made up my mind to no more mountain winters. Not much better wintering down there in the valley, so I believe I'll give Nevada a try."

"I'll be calling my sister's brother-in-law soon," Steve said. "I'll ask him to let my sister know about finding you a place."

Willa nodded. "Be a help, that would. One thing we all got to face, nobody gets any younger. Course, you two got a lot of young years ahead yet."

"We're hiking down to Hanksville after lunch," Victoria said. "Would you like to stay and eat with us?"

"Take you up on that quick as a snap, I would, but I got a woman coming up to get some herb drops from me for her rheumatiz. Said she'd be arriving today about noon so I'd best get back. My simples are good enough, but climbing up the mountain's good exercise 'n' I always figure that helps her rheumatiz."

Victoria nodded. Willa was using a layman's term

for arthritis and she was right about exercise being a help. Heaven only knew what was in her ''drops,'' but with herbal medicines gaining recognition today, it could be the old woman knew what she was doing.

Willa did accept a cup of tea and got to hold Heidi for a few minutes. ''You ever bring this 'un to see your sister in Nevada, maybe I can see how she's growing once I get settled there,'' she said to Steve.

''You and my sister will get along famously,'' he assured Willa. ''She's not like me at all.''

Willa grinned at him. ''You're not so bad on more acquaintance. Wear pretty well, you do.''

After she left, Victoria decided Willa was right on. Despite the reservations she, herself, had about him, Steve did wear well.

Lunch over, she inserted Heidi into the pouch and set off with Steve and Joker for Hanksville. Again the squawking jay followed them for a time.

''He's another early warning system,'' she said, glancing at Steve.

Though she'd managed to coax him from his dour mood yesterday, his talk of emergencies had made her wonder if he was still keeping vital information from her. Had his extreme reaction to the van being out of oil been based on something he hadn't told her?

Steve nodded, but made no comment to her remark about early warning systems, giving her no clue at all as to whether he might or might not think they needed more protection than Joker would provide.

Though the afternoon was warm and pleasant, Victoria's mood was not as easy and relaxed as the first time they'd made this hike.

Steve must have sensed this because he said, "Worrying about the climb back up?"

"Not really," she said, forcing lightness into her tone. "If I collapse on the upward trail, I figure you'll put on Heidi's pouch, baby and all, sling me over your shoulder and tromp on, complete with innumerable quarts of oil. Unless you're in your Bluebeard persona—then, who knows?"

He chuckled. "Even if I did grow a beard, it wouldn't be black, much less blue-black."

"No problem, you could always dye it blue."

With a woof, Joker took over into the underbrush after a chipmunk, causing a brief halt. Steve shouted, "Heel!"

After a minute or two, the dog reappeared, looking guilty and fell in obediently behind Steve as they walked on. After being told what a good dog he was, Joker's tail began to wag again and he bounded ahead.

Victoria caught Steve eyeing her assessingly and shook her head. "No way. Don't even let it cross your mind."

He grinned. "Why not? Life would be a lot easier for men if we could get women to obey a few simple commands, that's for sure."

"Women are not dogs to be ordered around!"

"I have to agree—they're more like cats."

Since cats rarely obey any order, she decided to take that as a compliment. Glancing down at the baby in her pouch, she saw Heidi had fallen asleep. Going on hikes must agree with her.

"I don't know much about them," Steve said, apparently having followed her gaze, "but she's obviously a wonderful baby."

"Top of the line," Victoria agreed.

They exchanged congratulatory smiles. Though neither of us can take credit for who Heidi is, Victoria told herself, we do keep her happy and content. She knows we love her.

Which brought back her jabbing little needle of worry about not knowing all she needed to.

"Steve," she said, "are you really sure we're not in any danger up here in the mountains?"

"Danger? You mean bears or mountain lions?"

"You know I don't. Are you sure there isn't more you need to tell me? If I'm operating blind, how can I tell what to do or not do?"

"In the world we live in, no one is entirely safe," he began.

"Don't give me generalities. I want specifics. Is Heidi safe up here?"

He took so long to answer, she thought he wasn't going to. But finally he paused and turned to look at her. "I honestly don't know," he said. "I hope so. That's the best I can do."

Chapter Twelve

Victoria carried the burden of Steve's words with her the rest of the way down the trail. He *hoped* Heidi was safe but he couldn't be *sure* she was. Why? Victoria knew asking would bring her up against a stone wall. Damn the man.

Before this she'd assumed the village was totally harmless, but now she felt uneasy about going there, about being away from the cabin.

Which didn't make much sense. If danger pursued them, the cabin wouldn't be safe, either. But did it? Steve had really given her no reason to think any of them were in peril at the moment.

Stop worrying, she told herself firmly.

Just before they reached Hanksville, Steve snapped Joker's leash on. As before, he stopped at the gas station pay phone. She was about to head across the street to the general store when Joker whined, pulling at the leash Steve held.

"He wants to go where Heidi goes," Victoria said, reaching for the leash, glad she'd have the dog with them to ease her mind.

"Good dog," Steve told him, handing over the leash to Victoria.

When she reached the store, Victoria tied Joker outside, telling him to stay. Inside, she located the baby vitamins, paid for them, then walked around looking for pads for outdoor chairs. She hadn't really expected to find any—Aylestown was a more likely source—and she didn't.

Since there was nothing else they needed, she left the store, retrieved the dog and glanced around. Her survey confirmed her feeling there was absolutely nothing in this sleepy little place to alarm anyone. Since Steve was still on the phone, she decided to stroll along the sidewalk toward the little park on the river.

At the end of the sidewalk, she stopped, suddenly nervous about going any farther alone. Even though she could see or hear nothing tangible to be afraid of, she'd rather be with Steve right now.

There was no reason to feel so exposed on this deserted sidewalk, but she did. Making up her mind, she said, "Change of plan, Joker," and tugged at the leash.

She stepped onto the weedy grass between the sidewalk and the street, ready to cross over to the gas station side to where Steve was. Noticing a car pulling out of the station toward her, she waited.

Instead of driving past, the car crossed to the wrong

side of the road, taking her aback as it pulled up beside her. Before she had time to react, a man in a dark jacket leapt out and lunged at her, making a grab for the baby. Joker snarled, yanked the leash from her hand and, teeth bared, charged at the man, who tried to fend him off.

The attacker let out a yell when Joker bit his leg. As he struggled to get away, to Victoria's horror, he jerked a gun from under his jacket and aimed it at the dog.

"No!" she screamed, flinging the package of baby vitamins at him.

The man flinched, but the gun fired and Joker yelped, letting go of the man's leg.

"Freeze!" someone yelled. Steve! With his gun drawn. She hadn't been aware he'd brought it along.

Instead of obeying, the man jumped back into the car and, tires screeching in a U-turn, roared off. Steve stared after the car for a moment, tucked the gun away, then dropped to his knees to examine the dog. Joker, licking his side, allowed Steve to take a look.

"The bullet just creased him, thanks to you," he told Victoria. "What'd you throw at that guy?"

"Heidi's vitamins. Oh, Steve, he tried to take her away from me!"

By now a small crowd was gathering, attracted by the gunshot. Undeterred, Steve hugged Victoria, baby and all, close to him. "Thank God you're both okay."

"Hey, mister, what happened?" a teenaged boy asked.

"Drive-by shooting, I guess," Steve said, releasing her. "Luckily no one got hurt."

"Whoa, you mean you didn't know that guy in the car?" the kid persisted.

"Never saw him before and neither had the lady. Must have been some kind of crazy."

"Lot of that going around," an older man said. "See it all the time on the news. Never expected such a thing in Hanksville, though. We ain't exactly what you'd call a high-crime area."

"If you'll excuse us," Steve said, "we'll be getting on. The lady's pretty shook up." He bent and retrieved the end of Joker's leash. The dog was pressed closely against Victoria's legs, obviously worried about the baby's safety.

The teenager picked the small bag containing the vitamins from the ground. "This your package?" he asked Victoria.

She took it, saying, "Yes, thank you," surprised she sounded so calm when her insides were still churning.

Her legs seemed to work all right, though, no matter how rubbery they felt, so she had no trouble keeping up with Steve as he urged her through the now-dispersing crowd. She was amazed that none of this had frightened the baby.

"Gonna see if I can find the bullet," she heard the teenager saying as she and Steve walked away with the dog.

He kept her moving until they reached the trail and the trees closed around them. Then he paused and said, "I'll take the baby."

Involuntarily she glanced over her shoulder.

"He won't follow us," Steve assured her as he donned the pouch while she held Heidi.

"How can you be so sure?"

He shrugged, inserted the baby deftly into the pouch, then gave Joker a pat, saying, "Good dog."

"Joker saved us—saved the baby anyway," Victoria said. "Whoever that man was, he had no interest in me. He wanted Heidi."

"I'm going back to pick up the oil I left at the station," Steve said. "You stay here."

Victoria swallowed.

Her expression must have given away her apprehension because Steve said, "He's long gone. Sit down and rest until I get back. We've got a long climb ahead of us."

"But—the baby?"

"I've got a gun—and Joker. There won't be a problem now, anyway. That scumbag meant it to be a hit-and-run kidnapping and he failed." Steve strode off, heading down to Hanksville again, leaving her alone.

She stepped off the trail, taking cover in the pines before easing down with her back against a tree trunk, not caring that the ground was still damp. How could Steve be so certain the kidnapper wouldn't return? He'd claimed he didn't know the man, but was he telling the truth?

She found it impossible to believe it was a random act. To her way of thinking, that man had wanted Heidi, not just any baby. But how would he have known the baby Victoria carried *was* Heidi? The only possible conclusion was because he'd seen her with Steve and he knew who Steve was.

He must have been waiting in his car in the gas station when they came into the village together. She hadn't noticed it at the time, but why would she? There were usually cars in a gas station. The would-be kidnapper's had definitely come from there, all right.

Was all this fact or was some of it a wild imagining she'd conjured up? She thought it was true. Even if it was all in her mind, though, Steve owed her some answers.

Quiet as she was, a squirrel overhead spotted her and began chittering, annoyed she'd invaded his territory. It occurred to her that, if an attacker listened to the birds and animals and understood their calls, he could find a person trying to hide in the woods.

No one's searching for me, she told herself firmly, trying to calm her thudding heart. By the time Joker came bounding up to her, she'd almost succeeded. She rose and, when Steve hove into view, carrying a bag with what must be the oil cans, she made her way back to the trail.

As they started up, she said, "We need to talk about—"

Steve cut her off. "Save your breath for the climb. I intend to."

It irked her that he was probably right. She didn't want to wait, she wanted answers now. But she subsided, aware she wasn't likely to get any until he decided the time was right.

It was nearing dusk when they reached the cabin. Heidi needed to be changed and fed and so she took care of that while Steve poured oil into the van. When the baby was settled in the cradle, Victoria cornered Joker outside and took a careful look at his side. A crease, Steve had called it—accurately as far as she could tell—because the bullet had barely broken the dog's skin and there was hardly any bleeding. To Joker's obvious disgust, she washed the shallow injury with soap and water to be on the safe side.

"What a brave dog, you are," she told him as she finished and turned him loose.

He went right back to licking his wound.

She walked over to Steve who was still fooling around underneath the van's hood. "Everything okay?"

He glanced up, frowning. "Nothing wrong I can find. Providing I got the oil into her in time, she'll take us down the mountain and beyond. Damn that malfunctioning warning light."

Victoria stared at him from the other side of the van. "Are you telling me we're leaving here for good right now?"

"First thing in the morning. We'll pack tonight."

"Then it *was* Heidi he was after."

Steve slammed down the hood.

"If you meant that as a warning to shut up," Victoria continued, "you may as well forget it. You owe me information. What happened today scared me half to death. How can I try to protect the baby when I'm totally in the dark as to what's going on?"

He jerked his head toward the chairs in front of the cabin and they headed for them. "I don't like the idea of leaving tonight," he said as they sat down. "The dark makes it hard to spot danger."

"What danger?"

"I made another phone call when I picked up the oil. A helicopter will arrive in the morning. There's no clearing for it to set down up here so we have to drive to Aylestown.''

Victoria took a deep breath and let it out slowly. ''Don't confuse me with helicopters. Start at the beginning. Who was that man Joker bit?''

''Don't know him personally, but I do know he works for Heidi's father. What I can't figure out is how Malengo got onto the fact we were somewhere near Hanksville. You couldn't have let anything slip because you haven't been near a phone.''

Though, anatomically, hearts can't sink, Victoria had the dismal sensation hers was doing just that. ''I—uh—did send a letter from the Hanksville post office about my mail along with the key to Alice a few days ago,'' she admitted.

Steve came halfway out of his chair. ''You what?''

She bristled. ''How was I to know that was dangerous? If you weren't so closemouthed—''

''Alice being your psychologist apartment neighbor?'' he asked.

She nodded. ''But—''

''It wouldn't have been hard for them to find out you were the nurse who left the hospital with me and the baby. Once they had your name, it'd be a snap to locate your apartment. Which they did do, because they were waiting there when I retrieved your medical kit from your car. They followed me. I lost the tail. But that's why we came to the cabin—because it was only a matter of time before we were no longer safe in the town house.''

''Alice wouldn't tell anyone where—''

''How about a fake 'postal inspector'?''

Victoria blinked. ''That sounds so—so organized.''

"Malengo's one of the crime kingpins. Unfortunately we haven't managed to nail him with a specific count yet."

"Oh, no!" Victoria's hand flew to her mouth. "Are you telling me Heidi's father is some kind of master criminal?"

"Bingo. With all sorts of connections."

"And now that his flunky has seen us in Hanksville, you think he'll find the cabin, find us, if we don't get away. Am I right?"

"More or less. In the light of today's happenings, people in the village are going to be leery of talking to strangers so it'll take him time to learn about the two cabins up here. We're safe enough tonight, but no longer. Sooner or later he'll find out which cabin is Willa's, so that'll pinpoint us. In the morning, as soon as it's light, we're off."

Victoria took a deep breath, doing her best to assimilate all this. "Kim ran off with a man she knew was a criminal?" she asked finally.

"Kim was good at denial—she had a tendency to accept only what she wanted to hear. I can't be sure, but my take on it is that she didn't fully realize what he was until after she got pregnant. Something must have unrolled in front of her that she couldn't help seeing, want to or not."

Victoria nodded. "What you're saying is Kim wanted her baby but she didn't want a criminal raising the child."

"That's how I call it. Kim was a good-looking woman, but Malengo had an ulterior motive in acquiring her. He knew who I was and he thought she might be a source of info about the agency."

"Through you? Closemouthed Steve?"

"I didn't say he got much, if anything."

"Oh, poor Kim. To give someone like you up for a—" Victoria paused as she realized what she was saying and flushed. Good grief, next she'd be admitting she loved him.

Damn it, she didn't. Did she? How could she love a man who couldn't trust her enough to tell her the truth right from the beginning? Who even now was probably only feeding her bits and pieces?

Steve gave her a wry grin. "Yeah, even in my Bluebeard persona, as you call, I'm no scumbag."

"I guess I'd better start packing," she said.

"Good idea. You'll be leaving most of your things in the van, we'll load them in tonight. In the morning, the agency helicopter will pick you and Heidi up in Aylestown. You'll only be able to take necessities on the flight."

She stared at him. "What about you?"

"I'll stick with the van."

"But what if—?"

"They want Heidi, not me." His voice turned grim. "And they bloody well aren't going to get her. *Or* you."

"Where are we being taken?"

"To a safe place. I'll join you when I can and we'll sort things out then."

"Sort things out? What things?"

He rose from the chair. "Like you said, better start packing."

She'd been told all he thought she needed to hear, Victoria thought, refusing to give way to annoyance. This was no time to fume over Steve's inability to share information, even though she was sure not everything was classified and he could have told her more had he chosen to.

Later, with everything they didn't need for immediate use packed in boxes and loaded into the van, Victoria decided to clean out the refrigerator for their evening meal. She was peering into it, muttering to herself, "Eggs, bacon, butter," when Steve came up behind her.

"Did I hear bacon and eggs?" he asked. "Sounds like my kind of supper. I'll do my thing with them again."

"Never let it be said that I stood in the way of a true chef," Victoria told him, sounding far more lighthearted than she felt.

This may be the next to last meal we eat together, she thought as she set the table. There'll be a breakfast of sorts and then—what?

The future stretched ahead, unknowable for the moment but a future she was almost positive wouldn't include Steve. Or Heidi. She bit her lip to keep tears from forming.

Once the meal was over, they shared the cleaning up until Heidi began to fuss. Almost simultaneously each said, "I'll take care of her."

Victoria and Steve stared at one another, something intangible passing between them, felt but impossible to identify. A *she's ours* bond? Or that and more?

"Go ahead," Steve said finally. "I still have to clobber together some kind of a carrier for Bevins so he won't be all over us in the van."

As he watched Victoria lift the baby from the cradle and hold her close, a lump came into his throat.

How was he going to be able to give up what they'd had here in the cabin? The divorce from Kim had been a quick ax chop—not painless, but quick to heal.

What was between him and Victoria wouldn't be easily forgotten. He might be able to find a way to keep Heidi but Victoria was her own free agent. Though he'd come to love the baby, without Victoria it wouldn't be the same.

Nothing would be the same without her.

Pull yourself together, Henderson, he warned himself. You still have to get them to safety—concentrate on that.

Leave tonight? He shook his head. Waiting for the chopper was the safest for Victoria and the baby. If he took off now with them in the van, they might well be intercepted between here and Maryland, with a possible shoot-out.

He doubted Malengo could assemble enough men to attack the cabin and get them up here from Maryland, until some time tomorrow. In any case, Malengo had to find the cabin, and that was easier done by daylight.

Not that Steve expected to sleep much tonight.

As he finished up in the kitchen, he all but tripped over Joker who was obviously looking for a handout. Steve had scraped all the leftovers together onto a piece of aluminum foil and, breaking his rule of never feeding the dog in the kitchen, he set foil and all on the floor.

Joker gave him one disbelieving look before gobbling everything down fast, before Steve changed his mind.

"I'm counting on you to be our watchdog tonight," Steve told him.

When he finished putting together a crude cat carrier, he tested it by shoving Bevins inside, to the cat's obvious displeasure. Though the kitten pawed at the release lever, it held. Satisfied Bevins couldn't work his way out, Steve released him. What he was going to do with the cat and the dog, he didn't yet know, but he sure as hell didn't intend to abandon them.

After tying Joker outside, he settled into his chair, but instead of reading, he watched Victoria playing with the baby and marveled at how much they resembled one another.

"No wonder that woman in the general store took you for mother and daughter," he said. "Anyone would."

Victoria didn't answer, turning her face from him. He rose, crossed to the rocker and saw tears on her cheeks.

"How can I give her up?" she said brokenly.

He reached for Heidi, doing his best to swallow the damn lump that had returned to his throat. After depositing the baby in the cradle, he took Victoria's hand, pulled her up from the rocker and wrapped his arms around her.

He held her while she wept, patting her back and trying to tell her everything would be all right. The words refused to work their way past the lump, and so he was reduced to making soothing sounds.

How can I give her up? he asked himself.

The question haunted him even after Victoria stopped crying, pulled away and said, "I have to wash my face."

When she came out, he said, "We still have tonight together."

She stopped and gazed at him in silence, waiting, it seemed, for more.

"We need tonight together," he added.

Still she waited.

"I need to spend tonight with you," he said finally.

Victoria smiled encouragingly but didn't move.

He pulled at an imaginary beard. "Would the beautiful maiden I see before me dare to venture into Bluebeard's embrace? Would milady care to share a night with him?"

"Why, Sir Bluebeard," she replied, "I thought you'd never ask."

He reached out and hugged her to him, then let her go reluctantly. Bevins was prowling around and Heidi was still awake. Best to wait until cat and baby were bedded down for the night to avoid interruptions.

And they'd use the downstairs bedroom. He was fairly confident Malengo wouldn't surprise them but, on the odd chance he might be wrong, the loft was not the place to be tonight.

As if she knew he wanted her to go to sleep and was teasing him, Heidi cooed, made bubbly sounds and waved her hands and feet in the air. Steve lifted her from the cradle and stretched out on the floor with the baby lying facedown on his stomach.

"Look how well she can hold her head up now," he said to Victoria.

"Yes, she's growing before our very eyes."

"Got a long way to go yet, haven't you, blue eyes?" he told the baby.

Bevins padded over to check out this new situation.

He sniffed at Heidi, then climbed onto Steve's chest and began licking the baby's hair down flat to her scalp.

"Hey, she's not a cat," Steve protested.

Bevins gave him a-lot-you-know look and continued his grooming until Steve plucked him off and sat up, shifting Heidi to his shoulder. She promptly burped and spit up a bit of curdled formula onto his shirt.

"You're my messy little girl," he told her.

Victoria smiled at the fondness in his voice. Steve loved Heidi and would keep her safe. Or as safe as he could. She sighed, not wanting to condemn a dead woman for making a mess of things. It was difficult not to blame Kim but, after all, once Kim had learned the truth about Heidi's father, she'd done her best to escape with her as yet unborn child.

How Steve had changed since the baby came into his life! And what a tragedy it would be for him and for Heidi if he was unable to keep her.

I'm positively not going to get all weepy again, she told herself firmly.

Keeping any melancholy from her voice, she said, "So you see Heidi survived her first encounter with a cat, after all."

"I'm not any too sure he thought she was human," Steve said.

With knees bent, he now had the baby propped against his thighs and was making faces at her. She smiled at him once and then her eyes began to droop shut. Victoria walked over and held out her arms. Steve handed Heidi over and, after making sure the baby was dry, she settled her into the cradle and rocked it gently back and forth until, as Willa would say, Mr. Sandman came.

When she turned around, Steve was standing behind her. "I've taken care of Bevins for the night," he said, "so we're temporarily sans baby and cat."

The implication in his words made her tingle with anticipation but, at the same time, for some reason she felt absurdedly shy.

Steve took her hand and raised it to his lips. Her heart melted. And when he kissed her palm, running his tongue up between the webs of her fingers, the rest of her melted, as well.

"I remember when you hurt your shoulder," he said, "and I had to take off your shirt. It made me want to undress you all the way. Which is what I intend to do right now."

"Not unless we get to take turns," she said. "That's only fair."

"What's all this fair play business?"

"Equal rights."

"Whoa, heavy artillery."

"A gal needs every advantage she can find when she's dealing with Bluebeard."

"Okay, I'm convinced. Do we toss a coin to see who goes first?"

Chapter Thirteen

Standing face-to-face with him in the main room of the cabin, Victoria smiled teasingly at Steve. "No coin tossing," she said. "I'll even be generous and let you remove your own shoes."

He promptly kicked his moccasins off his otherwise bare feet.

She removed her tennis shoes and socks, saying, "Pretty exciting so far, right?"

"How do you know your bare feet don't turn me on?" He led her to the couch and sat down with her.

Lifting her feet into his lap, he began playing with her toes, running his fingers into the sensitive skin between them.

"That tickles," she said, giggling.

He slid his hands around first one of her feet, then

the other, massaging his way from toes to heel and back. She sighed with pleasure, closing her eyes.

"My intent isn't to put you to sleep," he said.

"It's just that what you're doing feels so good."

He continued his massage, finally saying, "What about some kind of exchange here?"

Victoria opened her eyes. "Ever had your feet massaged?"

"It'll be a first."

"Get ready for the thrill of a lifetime." She scooted to the end of the couch to give him room to swing his feet up into her lap.

"We start here," she told him, sliding her thumb and two fingers to either side of his left big toe. "Each toe on each foot has its turn before we go on to the ball of the foot, then the arch, then the heel."

"Who's this 'we'?"

"It's the nurse 'we,' which I really hate, but use once in a while just the same." She continued her massage as she spoke, smiling when she saw him close his eyes.

After a time he murmured, "If this goes on, you're going to put me to sleep and that's not quite what I had in mind."

"Really?"

In answer he swung his feet down to the floor, rose and pulled her up with him. Sliding an arm around her waist, he led her into the bedroom.

"You're leaving the lamps on," she said.

"Right. That's so I get to see what you look like for a change."

Without asking whose turn it was, he unzipped her jeans and slid them down her legs, easing her part way onto the bed so he could pull them all the way off. Before she could move, he ran his fingers up her bare legs until he reached the barrier of her panties, then caressed her through the silky cloth. By the time he let her stand up, she was thoroughly aroused.

She undid his belt buckle and, leaving the ends dangling, unzipped his fly, noting with anticipation the telltale bulge she had to ease over. When he tried to help her get the jeans off, she swatted him.

"No fair." As she spoke, she let her fingers brush against his arousal.

When his jeans were down around his ankles, she pushed him backward so that he fell partly onto the bed, in much the same position she'd been in. After yanking off the jeans, she slid her hand under the bottom of his shorts and caressed him until he groaned. He reached for her hand, moved it away and stood.

"Keep that up and we'll have a quick, one-sided trip," he said huskily.

He reached for her shirt and pulled it over her head and off before cupping her breasts in his hands. "You're so beautiful, Victoria," he murmured as he bent to taste them.

The feel of his tongue circling her nipples made her arch to him as waves of pure sensation rippled through her.

"My turn," she managed to gasp.

He lifted his head and she tugged at his shirt until it was off. Pressing her palms to his chest, she felt for his tiny male nipples and rubbed them between her thumbs and forefingers.

His arms wrapped around her, gripping her tightly

as he found her mouth in a devastating kiss that rocked her to the soles of her feet. She needed this man in a way she'd never expected to need any man. She ached for him, longed for him, wanted him.

She loved him. Whether he was the right man for her or not, he was the one she'd chosen without understanding that's what she was doing. And now it was too late to draw back.

But not too late to lose herself in his embrace, to savor each caress, to make this passionate journey with him into blissful forgetfulness....

Steve hadn't meant to fall into a deep sleep. On the job he'd trained himself to take quick naps, sleeping so lightly the slightest sound had him on his feet, gun in hand. But after the monumental lovemaking with Victoria, he'd dropped into oblivion so quickly, he hadn't realized it was happening.

Since, even at his most relaxed, he was never a heavy sleeper, he woke at Joker's first bark and was on his feet, adrenaline pumping, grabbing for his gun before the dog got really cranked up.

Since the noise was clearly coming from the front—Joker'd gotten loose again—Steve doused the two kerosene lamps and hurried to the front door. The waning moon showed just enough light for him to see through the window a magnificent buck staring at the dog, who was evidently smack up against the door, because he was out of sight.

The deer turned and, tail high, trotted down the trail. Joker gave a few more halfhearted barks and subsided, making no move to follow the buck.

By now Victoria was standing next to him. "Was that a deer?" she asked.

"Yeah. Joker doesn't balk at attacking a man with a gun but he didn't much care for the looks of that buck." Steve opened the door and the dog slipped inside, trailing his rope.

"I thought..." Her words trailed off.

"You weren't alone."

Steve bent to pat Joker and tell him he'd done a good job before leading him through the cabin and out the back door where he tied him again.

"I don't think I can go to sleep after that," Victoria said when he came back in.

In the faint illumination shining in the window from the moon, he could see she was still naked, and his groin tightened reflexively. Everything about her was made for love. For him to love.

But not anymore tonight. He'd gotten too wired from Joker's warning to make any more assumptions about them being safe. He didn't dare to lose himself making love with Victoria; he needed to stay alert.

"We can stay up and talk," she said, wrapping herself in the afghan from the couch and sitting down.

"We've pretty well told each other everything," he said, instinctively backtracking. "Besides, I make it a rule never to talk while naked."

"The last I saw, your new pajama bottoms were hanging on a bedpost. I'm perfectly willing to wait while you retrieve them."

He came out of the bedroom with the bottoms on and relit one of the lamps, turning it down low before he sat across from her in a chair. "Might wake Heidi up if we keep on talking," he said.

"She slept through Joker's barking."

True. There was no sidetracking this woman once she had her mind set on something. "Want a list of my favorite foods?" he asked.

"I already know a lot of them. I'd rather hear what you have planned for Heidi once we're safely off this mountain."

"I wish I could be sure." He spoke from the heart. Unfortunately Malengo had a legal right to Kim's daughter, since he was the father, as blood tests and DNA samples would undoubtedly prove.

Victoria frowned. "You mean you're not going to keep her?"

"If I can, I will. It may depend on whether or not the agency can intercept what's being shipped from Kholi with the Arabian horses and then link Malengo to the operation. If that happens, he won't have a hope of getting custody."

"You said you'd never let him get his hands on Heidi."

"I won't. Not unless a judge rules otherwise. Which, in the worst scenario, could happen."

"To hell with legality!"

He half smiled. "With that attitude, I may recruit you for the agency."

She shook her head. "I'm not the type."

No, she wasn't. Victoria was far too open and trusting to make a good agent. At the moment, she was driving him wild since the damn afghan had little holes in the decorative squares, giving him enticing glimpses of bits of her bare skin here and there.

He stood and crossed the few feet to the couch, easing down beside her. Unable to resist the temptation, he poked a finger through one of the afghan holes and touched her nipple.

"No fair," she said.

"All's fair—" He didn't finish the quote, realizing in time where that would take him.

Just because he couldn't keep his hands off her didn't mean love had to be brought into the equation. Or would it be a mathematical proposition? If thus and thus is true, then the result has to be—what?

Okay, so it was more than lust—he did care for her. But love? He couldn't connect to that word. People said it all the time and didn't mean it. They didn't have a clue what love meant. Easy to say, difficult to live up to.

"What about you?" he asked, forcing himself to stop touching her. "Going back to the ER to work?"

She nodded.

At least he knew where she'd be if he wanted to find her once this was all over with.

"But maybe not for long," she said. "I've been thinking about heading west—California or Oregon— and taking a job out there. I feel it's time for a change."

Putting a continent between them didn't appeal to him at all.

"Do you like being a nurse?" he asked.

She raised her eyebrows at him. "I'd hardly do it otherwise. How about you? Do you enjoy your work?"

Not always. But mostly he did. Mimicking her, he said, "I'd hardly do it otherwise."

She made a face. "Okay, you're one up."

"With you, that's not easy. Did anyone ever tell you you're too acute for your own good?"

With an exaggerated simper, she said, "I prefer to think of myself as just plain cute."

He grinned. "That, too." Plus sexy as hell. If he sat next to her much longer, he'd be tossing caution under the couch and making love with her on top of it.

Given the present situation, that could get them both killed.

Hearing Bevins begin to meow pitifully, Steve got to his feet, trying to ignore his rampant arousal, and headed for the shed door to let the kitten into the room.

Heidi took that as a cue to start whimpering. Victoria rose and went into the bedroom with the afghan trailing after her, returned with her sleep-T on and picked up the baby.

By the time Heidi was cleaned, fed and burped, the eerie glow of false dawn lightened the night sky.

"Once we get dressed and load what's left, it'll be light enough to take off," Steve said.

After he had his clothes on, he made a grab for Bevins, planning to put him in the carrier. The kitten eluded him, obviously thinking running and hiding was a fun game. Once he finally cornered Bevins and popped him into the carrier he'd made, Victoria emerged from the bedroom fully dressed, carrying a small bag.

"You might want to come back up here when you can and take care of the dirty towels and linen," she said.

"When I can," he echoed, realizing how empty the

cabin would feel without her and the baby. Even if he did get custody of Heidi, it wouldn't be the same without Victoria.

"I wish we could take the cradle," she said. "It's Heidi's first real bed." She shook her head. "Why do I feel like I'm leaving home?"

He understood exactly what she meant, but didn't care to pursue the emotion. "Look at that brat cat working on the catch to the carrier door," he said. "Bevins is too clever for his own good."

"Don't forget Willa told us he was named after a banker." Her smile faded. "Oh, Steve, I'm going to miss her, rattlesnakes and all."

Will you miss me, too? he wondered.

Enough of this. Picking up the cat carrier he headed for the door. Once outside, he set it behind the back seat, carefully wedging it in between boxes with the mesh door side out so Bevins could get air.

Heidi's car carrier was already attached to the back seat, but he checked the connections to be on the safe side. Victoria's bag and his own could go on the floor. Joker would be penned way in the back, behind a barrier so he couldn't go leaping around in the van.

Everything seemed ready for takeoff once they loaded in the last few items, buckled Heidi in the carrier and themselves in the front seats. There was no choice; they had to go. He'd never found it particularly hard to leave any place he'd ever been, not until now.

Victoria came toward him, carrying Heidi. She handed him the kangaroo pouch, saying, "Put this up in front so it'll be handy when I need it."

He did as she asked, then went inside, collected the

two bags and the last box and set them on the floor of the back seat. Heidi, now in her carrier, eyed him solemnly.

"We're going on a trip, little girl," he told her.

Why he should feel a lump in his throat was beyond him. They were all still together, weren't they?

All except Joker. Time to lock the cabin, collect the dog and be on their way.

"Just be a minute," he told Victoria, who was standing beside the van, looking about herself in the dim light, as if trying to memorize her surroundings.

Skirting the cabin, Steve went around to the back to untie the dog. Joker wasn't there; he'd gotten loose again. Damn, he should have checked on him earlier.

He called the dog, long and loud, with no response.

They couldn't wait any longer; they'd have to leave without him. No doubt Joker would head for Willa's once he found them gone. Might be there now. He'd be fine; she'd take care of him, but it hurt to go without Joker along.

Victoria came around the side of the cabin. "I heard you calling the dog," she said. "Where is he?"

Steve shrugged. "The escape artist did it again."

"He must have gone to visit Willa. I'll go find him." Before he could protest, she turned and ran off, heading for the trail to Willa's.

"Wait!" he called. "Come back!"

She either didn't hear or chose not to listen. He watched her disappear around a turn, the trees hiding her from his view. Not the blue jay's, though. The bird's harsh cry told him the jay was following her.

"Damn," he muttered as he returned to the van. He checked on the baby and the cat and cursed again.

Heidi was fine, but Bevins had managed to work the
latch loose and open the carrier. He was nowhere in
sight. Since the door to the back of the van was open,
chances were Bevins was hiding somewhere in the
brush.

He'd always prided himself on his ability to keep
everything in order, exactly the way he wanted it. No
longer. Babies, cats, dogs and Victoria had turned his
well-ordered life into chaos.

Slamming the back door shut, he started to walk
around to the front of the van when suddenly he
stopped, listening. Very faintly he heard the sound of
an engine—someone coming up his road. He waited
a moment, hoping for the prearranged signal that
meant it was an agency vehicle. None came. Which
meant trouble was already on the way.

He flung open the front door, grabbed the kangaroo
pouch and donned it, then lifted Heidi from the carrier
and deposited her in the pouch. Supporting the pouch
with one hand, he took off at a dead run, heading for
Willa's.

As he raced along the trail, the sun rose, sending
slanting rays through the pines. He tried to decide
what was best for the baby. Leave her at Willa's? No,
Malengo's men would find her there and might harm
the old lady. He didn't dare keep Heidi with him; he
needed to be free to shoot if he had to. Best to pass
her on to Victoria when they met up and send them
off ahead, down to the village. Once there, Victoria
could call the cops.

He'd cover the back trail, making sure she and
Heidi got away safely. No one was going to hurt his
woman or his child. *No one.*

Ever.

How many men had Malengo brought along? Would he split them up—some taking the trail straight down the mountain from the cabin, the others taking this trail to Willa's? Steve nodded. They'd have to, without a clue to which way their quarry had gone....

Wait a damn minute. He'd had the keys to the van in his hand when he took off. Not now. He didn't recall ramming them into his pocket. He checked. No keys. Which meant he'd dropped them. When? A ways along the trail? Or sooner? No way to tell. Which meant Malengo might have a clue.

He'd better figure most, if not all, of the pursuers would be on this trail. Since Malengo had had to come through Aylestown to reach the road to the cabin, had he thought to send a man around to Hanksville to stand guard?

I would have, Steve decided. So Malengo did. Victoria had to be warned.

At that moment, Joker bounded around a turn in the trail, startling him. That meant Victoria must be coming. He slowed his pace slightly. As he rounded the turn, Joker now at his heels, Steve saw her.

She started to smile, then sobered. "What's wrong?" she said as they neared one another.

"You take Heidi," he said, stopping beside her. As they made the transfer, he added, "Malengo's here. We have to get to Hanksville. You go first. When you get to the village, watch for a lookout man. What you're going to try to do is take the baby into the general store and call the police."

"What about you?"

"Don't worry, I'll be somewhere behind you." He leaned to her, gave her a quick kiss and said, "Get going."

Joker stared uncertainly from him to Victoria, now heading back toward Willa's. Steve pointed and ordered, "Go." The dog took off after Victoria and Steve followed, loping now to let her get ahead.

As Victoria ran, she did her best to keep from jostling the baby too much. She'd never been much for praying except for an occasional plea that her sister was all right, wherever she was. Now she sent up a prayer for Heidi's safety.

Though she worried about Steve, she knew he was armed and could take care of himself—the baby was helpless. She and Joker would do their best to protect her, but they might not be enough.

When she neared Willa's, the old woman was standing beside the trail, waiting. Victoria stopped to catch her breath and let her know what was going on.

"Steve's enemies are after us," she said, condensing the story. "They're bad people with guns and they mustn't get their hands on Heidi. Steve's behind me. Please show me the trail down to Hanksville from here."

Willa pointed to her right. "Leave it to me. I'll slow 'em down."

Victoria hurried on, wondering how on earth Willa thought anything she could do would have an effect on men with guns. She hoped the old woman wouldn't be hurt in the process.

When Steve loped up, he found Willa at the door of the snake house. "Trouble coming," he warned.

"Armed men."

"Victoria told me." She gestured toward the cages.
"I figure my friends here might help your cause. You
and your woman take care of that baby—hear?"

As Steve jogged off, Willa's words went with him.
Your woman. No more than the truth. His woman, his
baby.

Whatever Willa planned to do with her rattlers, he
hoped it worked, but he didn't count on anything. He
could only count on himself.

He tried to figure how long it would take Malengo
or any of his men to reach the Y where Willa's trail
connected with the one from his cabin. It was a
shorter distance from his cabin to the Y than it was
from his cabin to Willa's cabin and then down her
trail to the Y. On the other hand, Victoria had a good
head start coming this way and so ought to get there
first. Should he wait at the Y to head off any pursuers
coming down from his cabin? If only he had some
idea of the number of men Malengo had brought with
him.

He couldn't see Victoria ahead of him. The trail
twisted and turned so much it didn't really mean she
was any great distance away. Glancing at his watch,
he decided she'd reach the Y in about fifteen minutes.

If Malengo sent a man or men back down the
mountain by road, it would take them nearly an hour
to reach Hanksville, so that shouldn't be a problem.
If he already had a man waiting there, that would be
a different story. What Steve had to worry about right
now, though, was pursuers on foot and how many
there were.

He hadn't wanted it to come to this, hadn't wanted Victoria put in jeopardy. Heidi they wouldn't hurt or kill. He'd be devastated if Malengo got his hands on the baby, but at least she'd be alive. Victoria was another matter. Malengo wouldn't think any more of shooting her than he would Joker.

Unbearable to think of Victoria dead. He did his best to eradicate it from his mind. As he pounded down the trail, he pictured his time with her, their time together. All he'd noticed about her at their first meeting at the hospital is that she had red hair and looked as tired as he'd felt. It hadn't taken long for her to make much more of an impression than that, though.

Victoria was nobody to order around, as he'd quickly discovered. She stuck up for her rights—annoying at first but, as he'd had to admit, admirable. He'd begun to notice her as a woman that first night at his town house when Heidi woke them both up in the middle of the night. What man could fail to be attracted to someone so attractively packaged?

It had taken him longer to appreciate her inner beauty. He wasn't sure exactly when he progressed from simple lust to a more complicated emotion. When was it he realized that he'd give his life to save hers?

Which he hoped to hell wouldn't happen.

When the Y came into view, he slowed, stepping off the trail to make his way as quietly as he could through the trees until he reached the connection. He waited a few minutes and was about to step back onto the trail and continue on down, when he heard the protesting squawk of a jay from somewhere up the trail from where he hid. Since he knew the bird hadn't spotted him, the jay must be warning all within earshot of another intruder. Steve stayed where he was.

Victoria had been relieved when she came to the Y. As she remembered, the village wasn't too far from here. Luckily, since her pace had slowed considerably. Downhill was all very well, but she'd been jogging rather than walking and she was getting tired. Thank heaven Heidi hadn't seemed to mind the jostling.

Joker had been ranging ahead, but once past the Y she ordered him to heel and was relieved when he obeyed. It wouldn't do for him to pop out of the woods at the end of trail and advertise their presence before she had a chance to reconnoiter a bit.

The thinning of the trees warned of the trail's end before she reached it. She eased off the trail into the pines, working her way to where she had a view of the village with still enough cover to hide her and the dog.

Everything seemed as placid as usual but she took her time scanning everything. She eyed the car parked by the gas station. Was it the same car she'd seen there before, the would-be kidnapper's car? She couldn't be sure. There was a man inside it, sort of slouched down behind the wheel. He could simply be waiting for someone who was shopping in the general store, or he could be Malengo's lookout.

Since there was no way to tell, she had to find a way to get across the street to the store without him recognizing her. Offhand, that didn't seem possible. If he was Malengo's man, she'd be spotted for who she was immediately—a redhead carrying a baby, trailed by a most distinctive looking dog, one he wasn't likely to forget.

Time was of the essence; she couldn't go on dawdling in the trees. What to do?

In her jacket pocket, she found a scarf. Okay, head covering. But what to do about Heidi and Joker? She might be able to get the dog to stay behind but the baby was likely to give her away. Finally she came up with an idea.

First she tied the scarf in a turban arrangement that completely covered her hair. Then she took off her jacket and undid the pouch. She carefully arranged it, baby and all, over one arm, before covering Heidi and the pouch with her jacket.

"Sit and stay," she ordered Joker, in the sternest voice she could command.

He whined when he saw her edging from the trees but remained where he was. Taking a deep breath, she let it all out, then, heart thumping in her chest, stepped onto the trail and walked boldly toward the village street.

Chapter Fourteen

Once Victoria reached the road, she forced herself not to dash across. With so little traffic, if she seemed to be in a big hurry, she might attract the attention of the man in the car parked near the gas station. Though she didn't turn her head to look at him, she watched his car from the edge of her vision.

When she reached the other side of the road, she breathed a sigh of relief. His car hadn't moved and he was still inside it. She entered the general store, lifting her jacket off Heidi as she hurried up to the gray-haired woman at the cash register.

"Please call the police," she begged. "Someone is after me and the baby."

"You mean that guy over to the gas station sitting in his car?" the woman asked. "We already called the cops on him. Fred what works over there told my husband it's a different car but the same jerk that done the shooting yesterday.'' She narrowed her eyes at Victoria. ''You're the one he shot at, ain't you?''

Victoria nodded and thrust the baby, pouch and all, at the woman. ''Would you please keep her safe until the police get here? I'm going back up the trail to help my—'' She hesitated, unsure what to call Steve. ''My man,'' she finished. ''There are more than one of them and they're after him, too. Tell the police they're criminals.''

The gray-haired woman took Heidi into her arms. ''You got to be careful you don't get shot.''

''Whoa—you got yourself a gun?'' someone asked from behind her. Victoria looked around at a teenager carrying a fielder's mitt and a baseball bat. He looked familiar. At the same time Joker nuzzled her hand.

''I found that bullet, you know,'' the kid said. ''Saw your dog outside wanting to get in so I came in with him. Look, if you ain't got a gun, take my bat.'' He held it out to her. ''Better'n nothing.''

How much use a bat would be against a gun was debatable but Victoria carried it with her as she left the store. She cringed when she saw the man parked by the station already out of his car, ready to cross the street. Obviously he'd recognized Joker.

What to do? Her indecision ended when she saw a police car coming up the road. Malengo's man noticed it, too, and backtracked to his car, started it and shot out of the station, turning onto a side road. Lights and siren went on as the police followed him.

Reassured about Heidi's safety, Victoria ran across the street and plunged into the woods, heading up the trail. Nothing must happen to Steve! From somewhere above her, a gun fired, echoes of the shot reverberating from the surrounding mountains. A second shot speeded her pace, difficult as it was to run uphill.

He's all right, she told herself, her heart pounding from fear and exertion. The words echoed in her head. *All right. All right.*

Gasping for breath, she rounded a curve in the trail and stopped abruptly. On the ground just ahead, Steve and his assailant wrestled for possession of a gun, a mean-looking long-barreled weapon she knew wasn't Steve's. To her horror, she noticed a patch of blood on Steve's shirt.

He'd been shot!

Fury rippled through her, mingling with a roaring in her ears. She crept forward, gripping the bat handle, and began circling the struggling men, looking for her chance. The assailant shifted position, lifting his head slightly. She brought up the bat and whacked him. Readying herself for another go, she held when she noticed him slumping forward.

Steve freed himself from underneath the man, yanked the gun away and sprang to his feet, gun aimed at his assailant, who was now on his hands and knees.

"Freeze, Malengo!" he warned.

Malengo! As Victoria stared at the dark-haired man dressed all in black, she suddenly became aware that the roaring wasn't in her ears but came from a hovering helicopter. The agency to the rescue! When both she and Steve glanced up at it, Malengo leapt to his feet and plunged into the trees.

She grasped at Steve's arm as he started after Malengo but was too late to stop him. Why couldn't he let someone else, someone who wasn't already wounded, track the man?

Deciding she'd only get lost if she tried to follow Steve, Victoria also realized there was little point in waiting where she was. The best plan was to go down the trail to the village below, back to where she'd left Heidi. She'd gone no more than ten feet when a hoarse scream froze her in place.

What had happened? And who to?

She chewed on her lip, trying to make up her mind what to do now. Before she came to a decision, Steve erupted from the trees and she almost collapsed with relief.

"Malengo went over a hidden cliff," Steve said. "Don't think he survived."

"You're hurt," she said, staring at his blood-splotched shirt.

He examined himself briefly. "Not my blood. I winged him." He glanced at the bat she held. "Looks like I got myself one tough lady."

"The police are at the village. Was Malengo alone?"

"On our trail from the cabin, yes. The others took the trail to Willa's. She planned to toss her rattle-snakes at them. Serve them right."

Victoria shuddered and Steve put his arm around her. "Heidi okay?" he asked.

"I left her with the woman who runs the general store. Joker's there, too."

"Let's get ourselves down to the store pronto. The rattlers may have missed a few." A quick hug and he let her go.

The copter was hovering over Hanksville when

they reached the village. Letting Victoria go to Heidi, Steve stopped at the gas station phone and called the agency. "Let the guys in the chopper know there's a baseball field east of town," he said. "I'll make sure no one's on the field so they can set down."

Partway there, a teenager carrying what looked like the bat Victoria had used, caught up to him.

"Whatcha gonna do now, mister?" he asked.

"The helicopter needs to land on your baseball field."

"Whoa—way cool! I'll go warn the guys." The kid ran ahead of him.

By the time Steve got there, the few kids who'd been shagging balls were heading for the edge of the field while staring up at the chopper.

After a time, it settled down onto the center of the clearing. As it landed, a police car pulled up beside Steve. "You Henderson?" the driver asked.

Steve pulled his agency ID from his wallet and the cop nodded. "Headquarters got a call from D.C. We're here for whatever assistance you need."

As briefly as he could, Steve told them about Malengo's fall from the cliff and the possibility some of his men were still on the mountain trail.

"You'll need to escort the red-haired woman in the general store with the baby so she gets here safely," he finished.

The police car pulled away and Steve headed out to the chopper, followed by the kids who'd been using the field. Whatever happened after this, he'd have the satisfaction of knowing Victoria and Heidi would be taken to a safe place.

* * *

Much later, after the chopper had lifted off with Victoria and the baby aboard, Steve and Mikel Starzov, who'd stayed behind to help wind things up, headed back up the trail to the cabin, along with Joker and a search-and-rescue team.

Near Willa's cabin they found three snake-bitten men stretched out along the trail, none completely conscious.

"May have whacked 'em a mite too hard with that chunk of kindling wood," Willa said. "Couldn't help doing it 'cause I had to give 'em the antivenin and I knew dang well they weren't about to cooperate. Some got bit more'n once, you know. Scared 'em to hell and gone. Dropped their guns and went to howling and carrying on."

Mikel looked around uneasily. "Where are the rattlers now?"

"Them I recovered are back in the cages. The rest hightailed it. Doubt if they're hanging around very close."

"You've got more guts than I have," Mikel told Willa. "Snakes and I don't see eye to eye."

"Just gotta know how to handle 'em," she said. "Got my daddy's old shotgun to hand but never shot the dang thing in my life. Never figure to. You, though, I'd lay odds you're a marksman."

"Best in the agency," Steve confirmed.

After thanking Willa, Steve left the men to the search-and-rescue team and led Mikel toward his cabin, Joker bounding ahead.

"Weird-looking dog," Mikel commented.

"Smart, though. Highest canine IQ in the country."

"Somehow I never figured you for a dog man."

Before the call telling him Kim was dead, Steve had never figured himself as a man who attached himself to much of anything.

Just short of the cabin, Joker dived into the bushes and came out holding Bevins in his mouth by the scruff of the kitten's neck.

"Don't tell me that cat's yours, too," Mikel said.

"'Fraid so." Steve plucked Bevins from Joker's mouth.

The kitten promptly climbed to his shoulder and clung there until Steve deposited him into the carrier in the van, twisting the latching mechanism with pliers so it was impossible to open. "Gotcha," Steve told the cat, earning raised eyebrows from Mikel.

"And here I thought I knew you," he said, shaking his head. "A dog and a cat besides the baby. Plus that charming redhead with the missing sister."

"You got any off time coming up?" Steve asked.

"Two months, if they ever let me take it. Why?"

"I'll let you know." Steve retrieved the spare van key from its hiding place. "By the way, when they find Malengo and go through his pockets, if there's an extra set of car keys, they're mine."

Steve coaxed Joker into the back of the van, shut him in, then grabbed a clean T-shirt out of his bag and changed into it before he and Mikel climbed into the front seats. He maneuvered around the four-by-four Malengo and crew had driven up to the cabin, and took off down the mountain.

"Glad we don't have to stick around for the mop-up," Mikel said. "Bor-ing."

"I kind of like tying up all the loose ends."

"You're a neatnik. Me, I prefer the chase. Once that's over, it's all over for me. If I need to know more, they'll tell me what they found."

Steve glanced at him. "Same deal with women?"

Mikel shrugged. "Never met one I wanted to keep around more than a month or so."

"I can understand that." And he could. Because he'd felt much the same. He'd known almost from the day of the wedding that marrying Kim had been a bad idea. So how had he managed to get so hung up on letting go of Victoria? He had to, he knew that, but he didn't want to.

There was too much packed in the van to change it for the car he'd left in his rented garage so they continued on to Maryland, taking turns driving, accompanied by occasional outraged yowls from Bevins.

"We checked out your town house—everything's clean there," Mikel told him. "The boss thinks you'd be better off staying away from it, though, till this Malengo business is cleared up."

Steve nodded. He'd been planning to go to the safe house where Victoria and Heidi were anyway.

It was late that night when they reached the place. After they were admitted into the garage, Mikel helped him unload what was necessary from the van. Joker was let loose in the fenced-in backyard while Bevins came with them into the house. Steve left the cat in one of the unused bedrooms and went looking for his women.

Steve found Heidi asleep in a crib padded with bumpers so she couldn't poke through the slats. She seemed tinier than ever in such a large crib. He stood for a moment gazing down at her, relieved she was safe and sound and knowing he was bound to this little girl for life.

Victoria was sleeping in an adjoining room but roused the moment he looked in on her.

"Is it all over?" she asked, sitting up.

He longed to sit beside her, gather her into his arms and hold her forever but restrained himself. "Might be a few lawyers shouting for a couple of months but, yes, it's essentially over. They tell me Malengo was killed in the fall. With him gone, it'll all unravel."

"I can't help but feel glad he's no longer alive to be a threat to Heidi. Surely you'll be able to keep her now."

He had to touch her; he couldn't help himself. Easing down onto the bed, he took her hand in both of his. "Kim had no close relatives so there shouldn't be a problem, especially since she listed me as the baby's father on the birth certificate."

Victoria smiled at him—his undoing. He wrapped his arms around her and kissed her hungrily. He was never going to be able to get enough of this woman. She returned his kiss with enthusiasm, but when he deepened it, she pulled away.

"Is that Bevins I hear crying?" she asked.

"Yeah, but he's okay." When he tried to gather her close again, she resisted.

"There are other people sleeping in the house," she said. "Maybe you'd better bring the kitten in here with me so they won't be disturbed."

He got up reluctantly and started off to retrieve the cat, belatedly realizing on the way that Bevins wasn't really the issue. She didn't want to make love with him. Why?

Turning on his heel, he went back to ask her. "Never mind the cat," he said. "What's wrong?"

She crossed her arms over her breasts. "We'll be saying goodbye soon. Isn't it best to start now?"

No skirting issues for Victoria—she fired both barrels. He gave her a lopsided grin. "I was hoping to sort of taper off, not quit cold turkey."

She didn't smile back. "We do things differently—you ought to know that by now. I'll make a list of baby care agencies in the morning and you can start calling around to find a caretaker for Heidi. We'll talk then. Good night, Steve."

He refused to be dismissed like a throwaway lover, damn it. But he did agree this wasn't the time to argue the point. Exhaustion dragged at him and he was apt to fly off the handle when he was tired. She must be bone tired, as well. Tomorrow they'd both be calmer.

"Good night," he said, and went off to share a bed with Bevins.

She was right, Victoria thought. He didn't really care about her, except for lovemaking. Wonderful as that was, she wanted—needed—more from him. It was best to continue as she'd begun and get away from him as quickly as she could. Over was over. Period.

She'd known from the beginning that Heidi wasn't hers, though that wouldn't help the heartache when she had to leave the baby. Steve had never been hers, either. How had she managed to let herself get so deeply involved? Because he'd changed, that's why. Changed from the order-barking button-lipped person she'd first met to an amusing, caring individual who just happened to be the sexiest man she'd ever encountered.

Not that he was ever really frank and open. Steve would never be a blabbermouth, that's for sure. But he'd learned to care for Heidi, even though he'd known from the beginning she couldn't be his daughter. He'd acquired Joker and even accepted Bevins. As for her? Victoria shook her head.

Maybe she'd been more than a convenience to him, but with Steve it was difficult to tell. Come morning, she'd do her best to find him someone to care for Heidi and then she'd get out of his life.

Because she had trouble falling asleep again, Victoria woke late. Heidi wasn't in the crib so she knew Steve would be taking care of her. Since he'd also left her bag in the baby's room, she decided to shower before she changed into clean clothes. Think of it— a hot shower. She'd almost forgotten what that was like. Pure luxury.

Yet she hadn't minded roughing it in the cabin. Now that they'd returned to civilization, though, being up on the mountain with Steve was already beginning to seem like something she'd fantasized.

She'd expected to find him or somebody in the kitchen but she was alone there. She poured herself a cup of coffee from the pot and slid a slice of bread into the toaster. Coffee and toast downed, she wandered into the living room. No Steve, no Heidi. Bevins, though, was curled up in a corner of the couch on top of a cushion. He jumped down and followed her as she explored the house.

Muted voices led her to a small room near the door to the garage. Inside, a TV news commentator was talking about the stock market. Steve was sprawled in a lounger with Heidi cuddled against him, both of them sound asleep.

Victoria stood watching the two of them, trying not to let tears flow. They'd been a trio she was a part of, but she was no longer needed and it broke her heart.

Bevins brushed past her and climbed onto the lounger. He sniffed at the baby, gave the top of her head a few licks with his tongue, then settled himself onto what was left of Steve's lap. Despite her melancholy mood, Victoria smiled.

Without warning, Steve woke, glancing around as if unsure of his surroundings. Seeing her, he nodded.

"What a bunch of lazybones," she said, trying to keep any emotion from leaking into her voice.

He looked down and said to the cat, "I don't recall inviting you up here."

"Bevins considers an empty lap—or even a partly full one—enough of an invitation."

Steve smiled at her as he switched off the TV with the remote control. "I'd consider a two-for-one trade. How about it?"

Victoria knew Heidi would probably make the transition from lap to crib without rousing. Bevins could and did sleep anywhere. As she considered this, she all but felt herself snuggling into Steve's embrace. Which was not going to happen.

She struck a pose. "I fear I must decline your over-generous offer, kind sir. Business before pleasure, you know."

"Business can wait forever as far as I'm concerned."

"I beg to differ. We need to find the baby a caretaker, and the sooner we start looking, the better."

He shook his head. "Wrong."

She stared at him. "What do you mean?"

"Sit down and I'll explain." He waited until she took the chair angled toward the lounger before he continued. "You still have off time and Heidi prefers you to anyone else. And why not, considering your attributes? I've certainly taken to them."

"Make sense!" she snapped.

"Are we a tad cross this morning? That's the nurse 'we,' in case you wondered."

Victoria gave him a reluctant grin. As usual, she found it impossible to stay annoyed with Steve. "Okay, what now?"

"The agency doesn't want me back in my town house until the case is closed. And I'm definitely not going up to the cabin for a while. Can't stay here indefinitely. They may need the place at any time. So the perfect solution occurred to me." He looked expectantly at her.

"Not *my* apartment!"

"No, even you can't stay there yet, same reason as me."

"But that's ridiculous."

"The agency doesn't think so. They intend to keep us out of our usual haunts until this entire Malengo bit is cleared up. Overcautious, maybe, but that's how they are. I've solved our problem, though. I twisted Mikel's arm until he agreed to take temporary custody of Bevins, and the rest of us will fly to Nevada. Joker'll love the ranch.''

"Just a tiny little minute here. Why Nevada?"

"I told you about my brother-in-law's ranch. He's got plenty of room. Wouldn't consider it if I thought we'd bring danger with us, but that's all over.''

She glared at him. "There you go again, making plans without consulting me. What if I don't want to go to Nevada?''

"You told me yourself you were thinking of relocating to the West Coast. Nevada's close. Zip over the Sierras and there's California.''

"I don't know...."

"Yes, you do. It won't be forever. Besides, you'll like my sister and brother-in-law.''

"I'm sure I would. That's not the problem.''

"Then what is? Heidi needs you.''

But do you? she asked silently. Can't you understand we need to end this, that I can't stand having it drag on?

The baby stirred on his lap, opening her eyes. She focused first on the cat, offering the oblivious Bevins one of her charming toothless smiles.

I can't bear to leave her, Victoria thought. Not yet.

"All right," she said abruptly. "For Heidi's sake I'll go.'' Even as she agreed, she knew she was making a mistake. Instead of going with him, she ought to be running away as fast as possible.

His satisfied smile told her he'd expected her capitulation all along. Annoyed, she spilled out some of her frustration with him.

"If you'd been honest with me from the beginning, we wouldn't have to be flying off to Nevada," she said. "If you'd bothered to tell me about the danger we were in, I wouldn't have sent the mailbox key to Alice and gotten us in a real jam."

"Think about it. If I'd done all that, you'd have missed seeing Nevada."

"I could have lived just as well without it," she muttered.

Steve shifted position to prop up the baby, causing Bevins to give him an indignant look and jump down from his lap. "What would Alice the psychologist have to say about all this?" he asked.

"Probably something about never trusting a man who tells you half-truths, 'cause sooner or later the untold half will smack you in the face."

He chuckled. "We're even now. That canceled my one up. We leave tomorrow."

"Tomorrow?" she cried. "I don't have any clean clothes and neither does Heidi."

"I brought the boxes of our dirty clothes in from the van—you can use the washer and dryer here. Come to think of it, mine need washing, too. I took our dirty clothes to the Laundromat in Aylestown when we were at the cabin, so it's your turn."

"Big deal—you had them washed, dried and folded *for* you."

"You mean you're not going to fold them?"

If he hadn't been holding the baby she would have shied a pillow at his head. And then he'd grab her and…

Enough of that. Fooling around was out, since it led to what she was determined wouldn't happen again.

"How long will we be in Nevada? And where exactly?" she asked.

"Northern Nevada. The Adams ranch—Zed and Karen's—is in the Carson Valley, forty some miles from Reno. Can't say how long we'll stay there, that's up to the agency. Which reminds me, I'd better call my sister."

He rose, handed her the baby and left the room.

At least he didn't call before he asked me, Victoria told herself. He doesn't take me entirely for granted—for whatever comfort that's worth.

She lifted Heidi to her shoulder, gently rubbing the baby's back. "Why did I fall in love with a man who doesn't love me in return?" she murmured. "When you grow up, I hope you have enough sense not to do what I've done."

Isn't that what mothers always hoped for their daughters? Do as I say, not necessarily do what I did.

But she wasn't Heidi's mother; she never would be. The tears she'd successfully blocked before filled her eyes and rolled down her cheeks.

Chapter Fifteen

Nevada surprised Victoria, who'd pictured the state as a desert with a glittery oasis called Las Vegas. Northwestern Nevada was nothing of the sort, with the Sierras to the west, still some snow on the peaks, and foothills to the east, the valleys lying green and productive in between.

The Reno airport with its lights-flashing, noisy slot machines was a reminder she'd landed in a gambling state, but by late afternoon they were away from the city, traveling south in the van Steve had rented, with Heidi's carrier safely strapped in back and Joker in a temporary pen in the rear.

"Inconspicuous," Victoria said.

"What is?" Steve asked. "Certainly not the scenery."

"This gray van, your four-by-four gray van back

East, plus the car you drove in Maryland is older and black. Like you don't want to stand out in any way.''

He shrugged. "In my job, it's better not to be noticeable.''

"I'll accept that, but you're on vacation now. I'd lay odds this wasn't a random choice, that you asked for a black or gray rental.''

"I'd say you know me all too well. My sister's brother-in-law, Talal, is the exact opposite. Every one of his cars is an exotic foreign make—and red.''

"Sister's brother-in-law sounds so strange, even though I know she married a twin.''

"Identical. Since Talal shaved off his mustache, you can't tell them apart until they start talking. Talal's the one with the accent.''

Victoria fell silent. When she and Steve had shared their few confidences, at first she'd thought he wasn't particularly close to his parents, though somewhat closer to his sister. Now she was beginning to realize though that might be true of his parents, he was very fond of his sister, Karen. Plus, it seemed, all of the in-laws he'd acquired when she married—his extended family.

It made her feel a little lonely. She and her mother were not close. She and her sister once were but Renee had been gone for so many years that she sometimes had difficulty believing her sister had ever existed.

"You're lucky,'' she said without thinking.

"Why? Because the one quarter I dropped in the airport slot brought back three? I'm not exactly a high roller. My take on gambling is never lose more than two dollars and, if you win before your stake is gone, quit right then.''

''For a man of action when it counts, I've noticed you tend to be cautious otherwise. But I was really talking about you being lucky because of the family you inherited when your sister married.''

''Sort of overwhelming at first, especially as the nieces and nephews proliferated.''

Victoria glanced back at Heidi. ''It's good your daughter will have all those cousins.''

My daughter. Steve tried out the words silently. He'd gotten used to thinking of Heidi as his baby, but hadn't yet come to think of her as his daughter. The last thing he'd ever expected to be was a single parent.

He looked over at Victoria, wanting to share a smile, but she was gazing out the side window at Lake Washoe. She'd been unusually quiet for the entire trip. He'd hoped she'd loosen up after she agreed to come to Nevada. Though that hadn't happened yet, maybe she'd be more like herself when she got to the ranch.

''What did you think of Mikel Starzov?'' he asked, more to get her talking than anything else.

''Ruthless.''

He blinked. Mikel was a dedicated agent, good at his job, a bulldog on a case—but ruthless?

''I don't buy it,'' he told her. ''Not unless you consider me ruthless, as well.''

She shook her head. ''You're not. You're someone who's learned to be tough. I think he was born that way.''

''Hey, remember he took Bevins in.''

"Maybe his ruthlessness doesn't extend to cats."

"He's a good partner. A good friend."

"I don't doubt it."

Since Mikel as a topic of conversation was going nowhere, he abandoned the subject. He really wanted to ask what it was going to take to get his moonlight Victoria back.

"I miss the cabin," he said.

She sighed. "The time we spent there is like a dream."

"It was real." He spoke emphatically.

That earned him a glance. "Was it? Time out of mind, rather."

"For a time we were out of our minds? No way."

He got no response. Now she was looking straight ahead.

"When I saw Willa there at the last, I told her I'd be sure to have Karen and Zed check out possible Carson Valley sites that might suit her taste and income," he said finally.

"I can see she might like this part of Nevada." Victoria spoke with the same sort of cool detachment she'd laid on him for the entire trip. Only with Heidi had she behaved like herself.

He'd never before thought of the trip from Reno to Zed's ranch as long but at the moment it was beginning to seem endless.

"What the hell is wrong with you?" he demanded. "If you didn't want to come, you should have stayed in Maryland."

She scowled at him. "You know perfectly well you deliberately pushed my guilty button by telling me you didn't want to entrust Heidi's care to some stranger for this trip. Besides, there really was no place for me to go until your agency allowed me back into my apartment. I could have called Alice to ask if she'd put me up temporarily, but no, they didn't want me anywhere in the complex.''

"For your own safety, damn it!"

Her grimace told him what she thought of that remark. He more or less agreed that with Malengo dead any danger was minimal, but by now he was too annoyed with her to say so.

"You made me come but you can't make me like it," she snapped.

Heidi began to cry.

"Now see what you've done," Victoria accused.

"We've done, you mean. It takes two to fight."

"I wasn't fighting!" she cried.

Fighting was exactly what they'd been doing but it was time to call a truce if for no other reason than they were upsetting Heidi. Ordinary conversation and Joker's barking didn't trouble the baby's sleep but their raised voices woke her immediately.

Since they were now in Carson City, Steve pulled off into a strip mall and parked so Victoria could tend to the baby more easily.

Doesn't this idiot male understand what the trouble is? Victoria asked herself as she changed Heidi's diaper in the back seat with the side door open. Steve had gotten out to walk Joker, so it was safe to complain to the baby.

"Your father has the vision of a bat—without the built-in radar. He's blind to the way I feel, he doesn't understand, he doesn't care."

Heidi waved her feet in the air and made squeaky little sounds.

"So, okay, he loves you, no question." Victoria sighed. "I do, too."

If only he'd let her go, back there in Maryland. If only she'd had the sense to take off on her own and leave him far behind. Her mother lived in Florida now, she could have visited her, difficult as it would have been for both of them because they weren't at ease with each other.

She suspected her mother harbored a secret wish it had been Victoria who disappeared instead of Renee, her favorite, and that it made her feel guilty. They'd never discussed the possibility because her mother's way of dealing with unpleasantness was to deny it existed.

"I try not to blame her for staying with my drunken father for so many years," she told the baby. "But we both think that's why Renee left home. You're lucky to have a father like Steve."

"Thanks for the kind words." Steve spoke from behind her. She hadn't heard him come up. "I was beginning to believe you had none left for me."

Joker leapt into the back seat, sniffed at Heidi, licked Victoria's hand and jumped back down, apparently satisfied all was well.

Victoria wished she felt that way. "I'm tired, that's all," she said, which was half the truth. "I think I'll ride in back with Heidi the rest of the way so I can tend to her if necessary."

Conversation thus eliminated, Steve finally clicked on the radio and settled on a station playing songs so old, she'd never even heard some of them before. But the music was soothing, which apparently was what he intended, and she half dozed.

Victoria jerked fully awake when the van pulled off the highway onto a gravel road. Peering from the window, she saw mountains in the distance and, up close, fields, then a low, rambling house with a barn and other outbuildings scattered behind it.

"The Adams Ranch," Steve said from the front seat.

He parked by the side of the house, next to a bright red sports car and a rather beat-up Jeep. Before she could as much as open the side door, a bevy of children ran toward the van, followed by a toddler doing her best to catch up.

She slid open the door and a boy and girl climbed in. "I'm Danny," the boy said. "Are you Victoria?"

She smiled at him, nodding. "What's your name?" she asked the dark-haired little girl.

"Yasmin. Can I see the baby?"

As Victoria lifted Heidi from the carrier, a child called from outside, "Danny, come see the funny dog."

Danny jumped out but Yasmin stayed inside, gently taking hold of Heidi's fingers. "We got twins," she said. "One's a girl and one's a boy."

Victoria remembered Steve telling her about—was it Talal's?—twins. If so, Yasmin must be his adopted daughter. When she failed to remember his wife's name, she realized she was going to have a lot of sorting out to do.

"Aunt Tee's gonna have a baby pretty soon," Yasmin confided. "What's this one's name?"

"Heidi."

Yasmin smiled. "That's a name from a book our teacher read us in school. That Heidi lived in mountains just like ours, with goats. Papa might get me one. We got lots of room where we live now. Come on, I'll take you in Danny's house 'n' you can see my babies."

By the time Victoria, holding Heidi, stepped out of the van, the adults were there. Zed and Talal she recognized right off—it was hard to miss identical twins, even if she didn't yet know which was which.

She was swept into the house amidst a flurry of introductions. Steve and the twins didn't come in.

Evidently seeing her confusion, one of the women said, "I know just how you feel. When I arrived here with Talal and Yasmin, I didn't know what to expect. You'll soon get used to us. I'm Linnea, by the way."

One pair matched up, Victoria thought thankfully. The blond woman looked faintly like Steve, so she must be Karen, Victoria thought. Married to Zed. Which meant the one with auburn hair was the twins' sister, Jade.

She glanced at the lone man and he smiled, saying, "You can call me Nate, Nathan or Doc—I answer to all three."

Jade's husband. All matched up now.

"We have an empty cradle for Heidi," Karen said, leading Victoria from the kitchen to the living room.

The cradle looked brand-new, nothing like the antique Heidi had slept in at the cabin. After Victoria eased the baby into it, Karen pushed a button and the cradle began to rock slowly back and forth.

"When Talal took our old family cradle for one of the twins, he insisted on buying us this new one. I'll admit it comes in handy for visiting babies.'' She gazed down at Heidi. ''Her hair's the same color as yours. How interesting.''

''Kim—her mother—had red hair.''

''I remember her as Francine but I know she changed her name to Kim. The poor girl never did really understand my brother.''

''I think maybe at the end she did,'' Victoria said. ''Kim knew Steve would take care of her baby.''

Karen nodded. ''I'd like to talk with you about it later, when we can be alone. I'm glad Steve had enough sense to choose someone like you.''

To take care of the baby was what Karen must mean.

The three other men came in then, laughing.

''Strangest dog I've ever seen,'' one of the twins said.

''Joker's the smartest one you'll ever see, as well, Zed,'' Steve told him. ''Look how quick he made friends with your so-called guard dog.''

''That mutt has never guarded anything in his life,'' the other twin, Talal, put in. Victoria caught his faint accent.

Good, now she could identify them.

Fatigue and jet lag set in during the cold supper and everything seemed a blur after that until Steve ushered her into the bedroom that would be hers. The cradle had been brought in and Heidi was sleeping peacefully inside it.

Steve left her with no more than a quick good-night, which suited her perfectly. She crawled into bed and was asleep before she had time to blink.

* * *

Steve woke to sunlight slanting in through the edges of the blinds. Nevada. No way to miss the brightness of that sun. He lay quietly for a minute or two, savoring being here at the ranch. His sister and the rest of the family had liked Victoria, no mistake about that. But then he'd known they would. Who wouldn't?

He rolled out of bed, showered and dressed, then made his way to the kitchen where Karen was stirring batter in a bowl.

"You're in luck," she said. "This is pancake morning."

"Everyone keeps telling me how lucky I am."

"Well, you are. Nothing else explains how you ever had enough sense to not only find someone like Victoria but to grab her before she was taken."

"I hired her to take care of Heidi."

Karen nodded. "It couldn't have taken you long to realize you'd found more than a baby nurse—I know I don't have a dimwit for a brother."

Steve thought that one over. Of course Victoria was more than Heidi's caretaker. Meant more to him. A helluva lot more. She must know that.

His sister smiled at him. "I could tell as soon as I met her and saw you two together that this time you really did know what you were doing." She put down the bowl and hugged him. "To think that the two of you will be raising poor Kim's baby does my heart good. Heidi's a sweet little girl and it's obvious Victoria adores her."

Somehow the moment had passed where he might have stopped Karen by saying, "Hold your horses, kid, you've jumped on the wrong cayuse."

Forget the horses, she was railroading him. No, she'd already done it. Or had she? Maybe he'd done it to himself. Just what did he want here?

Better get some air, Henderson, he told himself. Clear your head. "Going to take Joker for a walk before I eat," he said to Karen.

She slanted him a look. "That means I've thrown you a ball you don't want to catch. Better make that a long walk, brother of mine."

Victoria brought Heidi with her when she came into the kitchen.

"I've unearthed Erin's baby seat for her," Karen said pointing to where it sat on a bench next to the table.

"My seat," Erin said from her high chair.

"Yes, it was, but now you're a big girl so it's Heidi's turn to use the baby seat," Karen told her.

Erin, Victoria knew by now, was the toddler she'd seen yesterday—Zed and Karen's daughter.

"I sent my brother off to have a chat with Joker," Karen said. "Men tend to be dense sometimes."

"You won't find me arguing." Victoria couldn't help but wonder, though, just what Karen had said to Steve.

"Luckily dogs give good advice by not giving any," Karen added. "He'll come back enlightened. Poor Kim was a mistake. We all knew it before Steve caught on. Time does mature most men, though." She smiled at Victoria. "Even my brother."

"In what way?" Victoria asked, unable to control her curiosity.

"He picked you this time."

"But I—he—we're not—"

"Give him a few more hours, okay?"

Danny, accompanied by a compactly built small boy, ran into the room. "Pancakes ready yet?" he asked.

"Soon." Karen turned to Victoria. "Did you meet Tim last night? With the kids all over the place, I can't be sure. Tim slept over with Danny."

"Hi, Tim," Victoria said, trying to place where he fit in.

He smiled shyly at her and then came up to touch Heidi's hand. "Pretty soon I get to have a baby, too," he said.

So he had to be Jade and Nathan's adopted son, Victoria thought.

Her expression must have given her away because Karen laughed. "There *are* a lot of us and it makes things confusing, doesn't it?"

"You've got that right," Victoria admitted ruefully.

Karen glanced at the two little boys. "I'll call you when it's time," she promised, and they ran off. Turning back to Victoria, Karen said, "Steve's inclined to be closemouthed. How much did he tell you?"

"I know that Danny is the son of your cousin, now dead, and Talal. I'm rather confused about the rest."

Karen nodded. "Then you heard I was named Danny's guardian. Unfortunately, my cousin never did tell me the name of the man responsible for her pregnancy—all I had was a picture of him. When I came looking for Danny's father I thought it had to be Zed. At that time he didn't know he even had a twin. Confusion reigned.''

Victoria shook her head. ''I can imagine.''

''Eventually Talal surfaced and we learned about how the twins were separated when they were three. Talal was left behind in Kholi after their father died and their mother escaped back to the U.S. with Zed. She was pregnant at the time. Neither boy was ever told he had a twin. Since Talal had to go back to Kholi after Zed and I married, he left Danny here for us to raise. Then we had Erin.''

''I think I've got that sorted out. Talal then married Linnea, right?''

''They came together because of Yasmin and wound up adopting her when they married. After what they'd been through, we were all so thrilled they had the twins.''

''Jade is Zed and Talal's younger sister, isn't she?'' Victoria asked.

Karen nodded. ''We were beginning to believe Jade would never find the right man but then she met Nathan when they both stopped to help at an accident scene. That's how they came to acquire Tim—he's such a sweet little boy. Still following me?''

''You've made things a lot clearer. Thanks.''

Karen smiled at her. ''Now we're waiting for Steve to get smart.''

Victoria didn't comment, sure that whatever she said wouldn't deter Karen, who seemed to be firmly set on believing there was something between Victoria and Steve. Which there was—or had been, anyway. But not what Karen thought. Victoria repressed a sigh.

After breakfast, Talal and Linnea arrived with their nine-month-old twins, Shas and Ellen, whose lively antics distracted everyone. Talal escaped almost immediately, claiming he was off to find Steve.

Between retrieving one crawling twin or another from imminent disaster, the women discussed babies, which Victoria enjoyed in a mournful sort of way, unable to forget she'd soon have to give Heidi up.

To switch the topic, Victoria told them about Willa.

"Oh, I think I know the very place," Karen said. "It's fairly isolated but you say that's what she wants. Give me her address and I'll write her."

When Steve returned, Karen gave him the pancakes she'd kept hot for him. After he'd eaten, he went out to the rental van and drove to the nearest pay phone. He needed to talk to Mikel.

The day passed without him being able to spend any time alone with Victoria. She seemed to constantly be involved with one or another of the kids or the women. Not that he'd figured out what he'd say to her if they had been alone.

At least she was herself again, laughing and friendly. The way he liked her, the way he was used to her being. She was fun to be with, not only because she put her heart and soul into everything she did, but because she carried a joyousness with her. She loved life.

And he loved her.

The truth struck him with the force of a 7 on the Richter scale, knocking him off balance, setting his mind askew. When he finally came to terms with the idea, he realized he now knew exactly what to say to her when and if he finally got her alone.

As dusk eased into true darkness, Steve found the opening he needed when the kids finished the game of croquet Victoria had been refereeing. Before she could rejoin the adults, he said, "Joker misses you. Why don't you come with me while I take him for a walk? Especially since I haven't ordered you to."

That earned him a smile. "It takes time, but you do learn," she told him.

The cycle of the moon had gone far past its romantic phase, so he couldn't count on moonlight to sway her. Karen's side garden near the gazebo would have to do. He let Joker take the lead, aware from earlier today that the duck pond just beyond the gazebo intrigued the dog, and so that's the way he'd choose to go.

He'd forgotten how sweet the scent of roses was until their perfume surrounded them. "Sit," he told Joker when they reached the gazebo. "Stay."

The dog looked longingly toward the pond but obeyed as Steve led Victoria up the two steps to the gazebo and sat down with her.

"What a peaceful place," she said. "I could sit here forever and smell the roses."

He found it hard to blurt out what must be said, so he started with Mikel's promise. "I have a surprise for you."

"Will I like it?" she asked.

"Yes. I know you find Mikel Starzov ruthless, but he's the best agent in the business for following ice-cold trails with incredible results. As his present to us, he's promised to find out what happened to Renee. If anyone can, Mikel's the man."

"Renee? He's going to look for Renee?" Victoria sounded totally confused.

"You need closure, and whatever he discovers will bring you that."

"Closure. You mean maybe Renee is dead."

"No one knows if she's dead or alive. That's what's bothering you. You need to find out. So when he gets here you'll have to put up with him picking your brain for everything you can remember."

"Mikel's coming here?"

"I invited him. He's bringing Bevins."

Steve could almost feel Victoria examining this from every angle, the way she did with anything that puzzled her. He anticipated her next question.

"Didn't you say it was his present to us? Why us? You're his friend, not me."

Steve smiled. "I haven't gotten to that yet."

"To what? Just what are you keeping a secret from me this time?"

"In a minute. Listen, I think I heard a coyote."

A faint wail rose from the distant hills and he said, "Old man Coyote salutes the night. Or so Jade's Paiute tales go."

From much nearer, another coyote took up the call.

"How wonderful," she said. "I've never heard coyotes before. It sends shivers down my spine."

He took her hand. "You've never heard me say this before, either. I love you, Victoria. I came to the realization today that life isn't worth living without you sharing it with me. I want to marry you."

"I—I—" she began.

"Wait. Hear me out. I know I'm too secretive about things that don't matter. I'll try to overcome it, but to be honest, I don't know how much I can change.''

"Now I *really* have shivers," she said.

"The question is, do you want to marry me?"

"Be warned," she said slowly, "that I'll keep nibbling away at that secretiveness, but no matter how closemouthed you stay, I'll love you anyway. I can't help it. As for marriage, how else can we give Heidi a mother and a father?"

He pulled her to her feet. "Look here, milady, that may be a plus, but it's not the reason I'm marrying you."

"It's not? Whatever for, then, sir? I simply can't imagine."

Moon or not, he had his moonlight Victoria back. Rejoicing, he pulled her into his arms. "I'm not always closemouthed, lady of mine. Here's a sample of what you can expect—with more to follow. On a regular basis."

As he lowered his head to kiss her, a coyote wailed again. Victoria caught a glimpse of Joker raising his muzzle skyward and heard him answer the call of the wild.

Victoria responded fervently to her lover's kiss, knowing only Steve could evoke and then satisfy the wildness that lay in her own heart. He was her mate as she was his. Forever.

Chapter Sixteen

On a late morning in July, Steve dropped the last of the Sunday paper to the floor and stretched. Victoria looked over at him and smiled. "Lazy days in beautiful Vienna, right?" she said. He grinned at her. She'd gotten a real charge out of the name of this town in Virginia where, after they'd married, he'd bought the first house either of them had ever owned. His pleasure, at the moment, came from seeing the two redheads in the other lounge chair, his wife and their daughter. His two loves.

"Oh, oh," he said a moment later, watching Heidi as she squirmed down off Victoria's lap and toddled toward the couch where the cat lay sleeping. He shook his head. Either Heidi was immune to cat germs or Bevins didn't have any lethal ones.

Before she quite managed to get the cat's tail in

her mouth, Bevins got up from his sprawl on the couch and leapt onto its back, out of Heidi's reach, gazing down at her with that supercilious look cats are born with.

Victoria not quite successfully muffled her laughter and Heidi turned to glance at her mother. "Bad Bins," she accused.

"Bevins doesn't like to have his tail bitten," Victoria pointed out.

Joker ambled into the living room, leash in his mouth, and stared expectantly at Steve. Heidi took one look at the dog and toddled over to her father. "Walk!" she demanded.

"Why me?" Steve wondered aloud, aware Victoria would list all the reasons why him. It had become a family ritual they both enjoyed.

What he really wondered was how he'd gotten along before the two redheads and all these animals had burst into his life. It was as though his existence had segued from black and white into living color. He'd never expected to be so happy.

Victoria watched with amusement from the window as the trio made their way along the sidewalk away from the house. Heidi always insisted on walking by herself, saying "Me do!" until she grew tired enough to be carried, so Steve was hard put to accommodate the slow toddler and the eager dog wanting to go faster.

Though Steve still worked for the agency, Victoria hadn't gone back to work at Kinnikec Hospital. Instead, she'd taken a part-time job at a local community college as a nursing instructor. She found she enjoyed teaching and it left her more time for her family.

The Malengo business was now water under the bridge, Oni Farraday and the other criminals arrested and the Kholi connection severed.

Thank heaven the adoption was now final. Though Heidi had been theirs from the beginning, she was, at long last, legally their daughter. How life had changed in just a little over a year. Victoria had never truly realized just what happiness was until Steve and Heidi had opened her heart.

Bevins jumped off the couch and came over to rub against her leg. "Okay, you, too," she murmured, reaching down to pet him.

If only Renee...

Victoria cut the thought short. Mikel Starzov was out there somewhere searching for her lost sister. She chose to believe that he'd be successful.

In the meantime, not only Heidi and the cat and Joker were hers to cherish, she'd been warmly welcomed into Steve's extended family, becoming a part of it. She belonged.

And best of all was Steve himself....

* * * * *

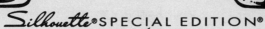

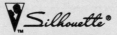

THE FORTUNES OF TEXAS

Membership in this family has its privileges
…and its price.
But what a fortune can't buy,
a true-bred Texas love is sure to bring!

Coming in October 1999…

The Baby Pursuit

by

LAURIE PAIGE

When the newest Fortune heir was kidnapped, the
prominent family turned to Devin Kincaid to find the
missing baby. The dedicated FBI agent never expected
his investigation might lead him to the altar with
society princess Vanessa Fortune….

THE FORTUNES OF TEXAS continues with
Expecting… In Texas by **Marie Ferrarella**,
available in November 1999 from
Silhouette Books.

Available at your favorite retail outlet.

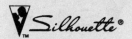

Coming this September 1999
from SILHOUETTE BOOKS
and bestselling author

RACHEL LEE

CONARD COUNTY:
Boots & Badges

Alicia Dreyfus—a desperate woman on the run—
is about to discover that she *can* come home
again…to Conard County. Along the way she
meets the man of her dreams—and brings together
three other couples, whose love blossoms beneath
the bold Wyoming sky.

Enjoy four complete, **brand-new** stories in one
extraordinary volume.

Available at your favorite retail outlet.

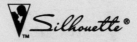

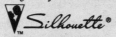

Silhouette ® SPECIAL EDITION ®
LINDSAY McKENNA
delivers two more exciting books in her heart-stopping new series:

Coming in July 1999:
HUNTER'S WOMAN
Special Edition #1255

Ty Hunter wanted his woman back from the moment he set his piercing gaze on her. For despite the protest on Dr. Catt Alborak's soft lips, Ty was on a mission to give the stubborn beauty everything he'd foolishly denied her once—his heart, his soul—and most of all, his child....

And coming in October 1999:
HUNTER'S PRIDE
Special Edition #1274

Devlin Hunter had a way with the ladies, but when it came to his job as a mercenary, the brooding bachelor worked alone. Until his latest assignment paired him up with Kulani Dawson, a feisty beauty whose tender vulnerabilities brought out his every protective instinct—and chipped away at his proud vow to never fall in love....

Look for the exciting series finale in early 2000—when MORGAN'S MERCENARIES: THE HUNTERS comes to Silhouette Desire®!

Available at your favorite retail outlet.

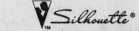